ABRA CADABRA

Harem of Freaks Book 2

CRYSTAL ASH

PROLOGUE
THE WOLF'S MATE

I ran on all fours, light as a feather on my paws. The thrill of the hunt filled me, lighting up my steps. Tonight my mate and I would find food for our pack. The pups inside me would be nourished with the potential to grow up to be pack leaders themselves one day.

The moon rose high, lighting up my mate's silver-white fur like he was made of moonlight himself. A fierce ache grew inside me, so strong that I let out a low growl of desire. I had to wait until we took down our kill, and then I'd let him take me.

We ran in tandem, following the scent of the elk herd. My dark, brindled coat blended in with the night and dry brush of the forest. Together, we were the same, yet polar opposites. Darkness and light. He would be the diversion, the last thing our prey would see. I would be the shadow they never saw coming.

Slowing to a canter and crouching low on our bellies, we didn't have to communicate the thrill and excitement we felt. It hung between us, crackling with coiled energy as it waited to go off.

The elk were resting, the large bulls surrounding the females and their young in a protective shield of antlers. But they were relaxed. They hadn't sensed us yet.

My mate licked my muzzle before slinking away to get into position. We'd done this dozens of times before. It was like a dance. A waltz of power, blood, death, and victory.

One of the bull elks' heads turned. Tension rippled through the herd as they watched and listened closely. Internally, I cackled with delight. They always fell for it. That was why they were prey.

My mate darted out and the bull elk charged with a furious cry. The protection broke as the males charged at their silvery-white enemy. Everyone began running and bucking in the chaos.

I chose my target, a young buck, and went in for the kill. Once my mate gave the bull elks the runaround, he'd helped me put our food out of its misery and drag it back into the woods.

Exhausted but victorious, we threw our heads back and sang to our pack. They'd hear our call and come feast with us. Other packs would hear us as well, and know to stay away.

We dug in while waiting for the others, eating our fill until our bellies were full and round. My mate gazed at me with his beautiful golden eyes as he licked the blood from my fur. With a snapping of bones, organs, and sinews rearranging, he shifted to human form.

I cocked my head at him curiously. He was still just as beautiful as a human, with pale, flawless skin, and silver-blonde hair falling past his sculpted shoulders. His golden eyes remained the same, set into a model-esque face with prominent cheekbones and an angled jaw.

"I want to take you in this form, my love," he whispered huskily.

I shifted to human myself so I could answer him. "It feels...wrong," I mused. "Not in a bad way, but there are no humans around for miles. This isn't the time or place for this form."

He shot me a naughty grin. "That's exactly why I want you out here like this."

I returned his grin. "You're so bad."

He pounced on me—clumsily compared to our wolf forms—and we both tumbled over, laughing and groaning at the forest floor poking into our soft, human flesh.

But when he kissed me, all the discomfort and feelings of wrongness melted away. His mouth and his body on mine awakened the animal side of humans we rarely felt. Nothing was wrong or bad about this. This was nature, this was pure instinct.

Our wolves growled restlessly just underneath the surface, frustrated at our dulled human senses, but we kept them at bay. This was a moment for us to enjoy each other as humans.

We often forgot that our human side was just as precious and intrinsic to us as our animal side.

MELODY

I awoke with a start, but the howling remained.

Perhaps my groggy brain hadn't completely come out of my dream yet, but that long, haunting song at the moon continued on until it gently faded away.

The coppery taste of blood still filled my mouth. I could still feel the wind whipping through my fur as I ran on all fours.

I never had a dream that vivid before.

Next to me, Connor's breathing was still deep, even, and human. He was warm and solid, wrapped around me snugly. I turned in his arms to look at his handsome, sleeping face. He looked adorable when he wasn't scowling at everything.

From the moment he found me sitting in the mud and covered in my own vomit, I never wanted to let him go. After being groped and manhandled onstage by my show partner, Connor was the only one who went looking for me when I ran off like a frightened deer.

I felt gross, helpless, violated, frozen with fear, and the

whole audience *laughed*. Syko touched me without permission because he knew he could get away with it. But Connor didn't let him. He made sure I was okay, then gave Syko a black eye for doing that to me.

As an eighteen-year-old runaway from the trash capital of Alabama, you could probably figure out that I wasn't used to people treating me kindly. Once I got a taste of that, I never wanted to let it go.

And not only that, I didn't want anyone to be treated like I was, or worse.

Connor shifted and groaned, his forest green eyes cracking open to slits as he gave me a clumsy, half-blind kiss. "Morning, babe."

"Morning." I nuzzled my head under his chin. "Did you hear that howling?"

"Nope." He rubbed the sleep out of his eyes. "You still thinking about the wolves?"

"I think…" I struggled to remember the dream, but it was already beginning to escape me. Rather than visuals playing in my head, it was more like incredibly vivid senses in my body. My sense of smell, hearing, and night vision had heightened to an incredible degree. It was like my brain was still human, but my senses were pure animal.

"I think I dreamed I *was* a wolf," I told him. "And I was hunting, then I turned into a human."

"Mm-hmm," he answered groggily.

"It was crazy vivid," I went on. "I could smell and taste everything, even the blood of the kill."

"Maybe you're part wolf," he said jokingly. "And that's why you can't get them out of your head."

"Maybe," I mused, kissing under his chin. "So what's the agenda for today?"

"Coffee," he grunted. "And breakfast. I'm almost out. We can get some from the vendors setting up today."

"When does the carnival actually open to attendees?" I yawned and stretched, life and awakeness finally coming into my limbs.

"Not for a few more days," he replied. "It would be smart to check the place out and get to know the staff and other performers. See if we're dealing with a bunch of Syko-types."

I mumbled my agreement and began pushing myself up to sitting, but he knocked my arms out and made me collapse back next to him.

"I'd much rather stay in bed with you, though," he murmured, kissing sensually into my neck and shoulder.

A hum of pleasure escaped me as I arched against him, sliding my palms across his broad, solid back. He moved lower ever so slowly, skimming his lips across my skin before stopping every so often to pay attention to a certain area.

Physically, we hadn't done much aside from kissing and a clitoral orgasm from his hand. I wanted to take it slow, and he was incredibly respectful of that. We'd only met last week and were still in the process of getting to know each other. I didn't even think he liked me until a few days ago. But with every kiss and gentle touch, I found it harder to not want all of him.

He was seven years older than me and every bit a man, not a boy, and carried the scars to prove it. Some mental, some physical. He was able to hide from most people that he was a double amputee, which didn't deter me in the slightest. If anything, it impressed me because he was a survivor. Not to mention an incredible acrobatic stilt walker.

I learned just two days ago that fireworks triggered flashbacks for him. Again, that didn't put me off in the least. I grew up watching my mother and older sister faking all sorts of disabilities to keep scamming the government for welfare money. If anything, it pissed me off that my own blood took money away from people like Connor, who needed it.

But whatever flaws he had were the furthest things away from my mind as his teeth traced my collarbones. His large hands held me by the waist as his mouth traveled slowly lower, between my breasts and then my belly, as he lifted my tank top.

My belly which immediately growled so loudly, it seemed to echo off the walls.

"Hungry, babe?" he laughed, kissing me there first before proceeding to blow raspberries.

"Maybe just a little." I smacked him playfully as I giggled and squirmed away.

"Let's get some food in ya." He smacked the side of my hip and promptly rolled up to sitting, using his arms to push himself to the edge to reach his prosthetics. Within minutes, we were out and walking hand in hand through the carnival grounds.

I never had a boyfriend before, despite having a few stupid hookups in high school. The way Connor laced his fingers through mine and held me at his side sent fluttering through my stomach that had nothing to do with hunger. Just walking alongside him, looking like I was his —and he mine—put an extra spring in my step. I had to bite the inside of my cheek to keep from grinning stupidly.

This carnival looked incredibly different from the one we ran from. Drowningville, Mississippi had been a shit-hole town and the Voodoo Trail Carnival was no exception, down to the people that ran it. Connor drove us off in the middle of the night after we technically kidnapped a family of wolf-like people.

Although I didn't give Connor much choice in the matter, the wolf family was being treated horribly and I'd get them out of there again if I had to.

I didn't know much about the people running this place, but Connor knew the manager and they seemed to get along well. I trusted his judgement above all else.

Already I found the grounds more pleasing to the eye than Drowingville. We were in the middle of a lush, green forest. The air smelled clean and fresh, with a hint of campfires and cooking food. I could see the Ferris wheel rising over the treeline. Spots of bright oranges, pinks, blues and other neon colors dotted through the muted tones of the tree trunks. Those had to be the other rides and the typical carnival game booths setting up.

Connor and I walked through an outdoor section where people set up simpler booths for their crafts, jewelry, clothing, and other goods. Rather than foldable canopies and tents, these people used colorful fabric held aloft by wooden poles. Some even used fur blankets and what looked like animal skins.

"Check out what they're wearing," Connor nodded at some of the vendors. "Looks like this is one of those Renaissance festivals."

He was right. Most people were dressed in costumes of another time period. Women wore modest, long-sleeved dresses like what I saw in history books at school. Men wore tunics and much tighter pants than I was used to seeing. Some even wore hats with feathers in them.

Even the food booths looked like medieval kitchens with cast-iron pots sitting over open fires. Animal carcasses on long spits were turned slowly as they roasted, making sizzling sounds as fat dripped down over the flames.

We stopped at a booth advertising fresh-laid eggs, baked beans, and the thickest, crispiest strips of bacon I'd ever seen. Even the coffee was heated over a fire in a metal percolator. Connor and I each got heaping bowls of food, huge mugs of coffee, and moved on, looking for a place to sit and eat.

Long picnic benches were set out under some trees, so we settled there and enjoyed our breakfast as we watched the rest of the temporary village come to life. Nearby, metalworkers and blacksmiths worked on their crafts and set up their shops as we watched with curiosity.

They set out beautiful wares such as knives, jewelry, and chain-mail fashion. Some were engrossed in making pieces, either by welding something tiny at their table or hammering a huge hunk of metal over an anvil.

Other people hanging around nearby were clearly performers. These were the ones we'd be working with directly.

I spotted a shirtless man covered in tattoos juggling knives by one of the shops. From his legs to his neck, he didn't seem to have an inch of un-inked flesh. And that flesh covered taut, rippling muscles that made his tattoos dance as he moved. His dark hair was buzzed short and even his scalp and the sides of his face had dark, intricate designs inked in.

He moved like a cat. Not that I knew anything about knife juggling, but he seemed even more skilled at handling them than Syko. I couldn't take my eyes away as he flipped knives through the air effortlessly as he chatted with the knife shop owner, often looking away from his juggling and laughing jovially at something his friend said.

Suddenly, he tossed all his knives up in the air at once and stretched his arms out to his sides. He leaned his head back and opened his mouth to stick his tongue out at the sky. Panic gripped my heart as the knives came falling back down to earth, blades pointing directly at him.

"Oh my god!" I screamed, covering my mouth as a dagger's blade gleamed in the sunlight before falling down his throat.

I looked around in a panic. Didn't anyone else see that? But all the shopkeepers and metal workers carried on like normal, paying no mind to this man with a knife handle sticking out of his throat. Wait, why wasn't he bleeding or moving around?

"Keep watching, babe," Connor said with amusement in his voice.

The man remained standing there with his head thrown back and his knife's blade down his esophagus. His hands closed suddenly, and I realized he caught two more knives which fell from the sky. He took a small step to the side and I could barely watch what happened next.

Another knife fell directly into his waiting mouth.

He then brought both hands to his mouth and swiftly removed the knives from his throat, still shiny and without a drop of blood on them. Then he winked at me and grinned as he took a small bow.

I covered my face, embarrassed at calling attention to

myself.

"He's good," Connor said with what sounded like genuine respect in his voice. "Really good. You don't see that blade swallowing stuff often anymore. Most people aren't patient enough to practice it correctly."

"That... was insane," I said, dumbfounded.

"Wipe your drool off if you're gonna keep staring," he teased, poking me in the ribs.

My face now hotter than cooking fires, I returned my attention to my breakfast. The knife-swallower guy was classically handsome, tall, and lean with a confident swagger. All the tattoos gave him a different, otherworldly appearance. From the way he winked at me, I got the impression that he liked showing off and even scaring people with his abilities. It got me more flustered than I cared to admit.

After breakfast, we explored more of the grounds with little incident before heading off to a private area of the woods to practice a new routine.

"Let's head to the bar tonight," Connor yelled down at me from high on his stilts. "That'll be the best place to get a feel for the people here. If it's shady, we'll cut and run after we get paid. If no one gives us trouble, we can stay for the whole event."

"Okay," I mumbled distractedly as I counted my steps, imagining I was waltzing across the stage. Honestly, I was excited about performing again. I couldn't wait to feel the energy of the crowd.

Just as I finished, a sudden, quick movement caught my eye, and I spun around.

A flash of white fur filled the space between the branches of the brush. And just as suddenly, it was gone.

2

MELODY

I was relieved to find out the carnival bar was in an actual building, not a tent. Despite how well-reinforced those pavilions were in Drowningville, I didn't put it past any of those wasted drunks to stumble into a support beam and send it all crashing down.

This bar was in a log cabin with a wooden sign sticking out from the side of the building with the word TAVERN painted on, along with a pair of drinking mugs. They were really playing up the medieval theme here.

Connor pulled open the heavy wooden door and stepped aside to let me in first. A smoky warmth enveloped me, adding on to the bright, cheery liveliness of the establishment. The warmth came from a large fireplace at the far wall, next to where a trio of musicians played a sultry background song on banjos and a standing bass.

"You want a coke, babe?" Connor had to yell in my ear over the music and multiple conversations. People laughed and talked animatedly like they were a few drinks in already. And the night had just begun.

I nodded at him, grateful that he remembered I'd rather not drink, and went to find us a place to sit.

"Thanks," I smiled at him as he set down two tankards in front of us.

He barely acknowledged our drinks or my thanks, but pulled me into his lap, trailing kisses down my neck.

"You practiced really well today," he murmured. "I'm proud of you, babe."

My chest squeezed as I balanced on his thick, incredibly muscular thighs, the main reasons he could perform so beautifully with no lower legs. His lap felt as solid as a table.

"I have a great teacher," I replied, wrapping an arm around his neck.

This was his first time being so openly affectionate with me and I wasn't about to question it. He made me feel like he was the first man I could trust, whose intentions I didn't have to question all the time. My feelings for him were growing deeper by the minute, and I wondered if he was experiencing the same.

"Excuse me for interrupting," said a lightly accented voice, with all the depth and smoothness of molasses.

Annoyed, I looked away from Connor and my heart jumped into my throat.

The tattooed knife swallower invited himself to our table and sat down across from us like we were old friends catching up.

"I feel I must apologize to you," he said. I couldn't place his accent, although it was pleasant to listen to. "I didn't mean to frighten you earlier with my knife practice."

"Oh, that's okay," I said, taken aback by his approach. "I should have known that was part of your performance."

Up close, I could see his eyes were a pale gray, like clouds after a rain. I could also see the finer details of his tattoos, including that he had small symbols inked near the outer corners of his eyes.

"My name is Razvan," he said, holding out a hand which had three eyes peering at me from his palm.

"Melody," I answered, accepting his handshake after a moment's hesitation.

He shook hands with Connor as well, but otherwise kept his focus entirely on me. It was unsettling, if a bit flattering. Connor's arm tightened around my waist and I laced my fingers through his.

"Where are you from, Melody?" Razvan asked, smiling as he took a drink from his own tankard. He spoke to me as if Connor wasn't even there, while I was still sitting in his damn lap. Clearly, his arrogance knew no bounds.

"Um, out of state," I said dismissively.

"Of course," he replied smoothly. "Beauty such as your own could not have come from a place like Mississippi." He said the state name in a mocking southern accent.

"Look, Razvan, I'm flattered," I said, growing impatient not only by his intrusiveness but also Connor's silence. "But I'd like to have some privacy with my boyfriend, please."

He smiled again, not looking put off at all. "Of course, I only wanted to apologize for making you scream earlier." The way he said it sounded so suggestive. I couldn't help but blush as he rose from the table. Which was most likely exactly what he wanted. Damn it.

"Boyfriend, huh?" Connor chuckled once we were alone.

"Yeah, sorry." I blushed again for an entirely different reason and took a huge drink of Coke to cool myself down. "I had a feeling he just wouldn't go away if I wasn't direct."

"Why did you want him to go away?" Connor asked casually.

I looked at him in disbelief. "Seriously? I'm in your lap right now. I was just kissing you. We don't have to use boyfriend-girlfriend titles, but when I'm with you, other guys should know to back off."

He took a drink from his mug and remained silent, the fireplace making flickering gold reflections in his dark green eyes.

"Why should they?" he asked.

I couldn't believe what I was hearing. I didn't know whether to be hurt or confused.

"Are you deaf?" I demanded. "I just told you. Because I'm with *you*."

"Mel, babe," he said with a long exhale. "I don't want to be known as your boyfriend, but not because I don't want you. Other men are going to be interested in you. If you hit it off with someone else, I don't want you to pass up happiness because you feel an obligation to me."

"I don't care. I'm not interested in anyone else." Was he purposely being dense?

"Really?" He raised his eyebrows skeptically and nodded his head across the room. "Not even him?"

Of course, he was gesturing to Razvan, sitting at a round table with a few guys inked up with similar amounts of tattoos, although none were nearly as good looking.

They laughed gregariously and spoke rapidly in a language I couldn't place.

"No!" I insisted, although my whole body heated to an uncomfortable degree. "He was *way* too forward."

"He's confident," Connor countered. "You gotta give him that."

"I don't want to give him anything. Why are we even talking about this?"

"I'm just putting it out there, babe," he kissed my cheek, "I can't give you everything you need. Someone else can probably give you what I can't. If you find that person, I won't be upset if you pursue something with them."

"That's crazy." I shook my head and took a long drink of my soda.

As much as I hated to admit it, I could see his point. Faithfulness was preached everywhere, but who really adhered to it? My mom always seemed to have a guy lined up after the last one left, despite her drunken rages about her dirtbag men always cheating on her. My older sister cheated on her guy just as much as he cheated on her. What did marriage vows really mean if you only said them because the church insisted on it for pregnant teenagers?

If people were at least open about it, was it really cheating?

My head swam so thickly with these thoughts, the raucous noise of the bar faded to a dull background roar.

Several boys had asked me out in school, and I even slept with a couple of them, but never expected it to progress to a relationship. Thanks to my mom, my perception of men was so skewed. I figured all they wanted was to stick their dicks in me and move on to the next girl. For the most part, I'd been right. Connor was the first one who challenged that notion. But now he was telling me he didn't want to claim me as his?

Whoa, where did that come from?

My thighs snapped shut as tension and heat suddenly built up in my core. The thought disappeared as quickly as it came, but its effects lingered. *Being claimed?* It sounded so raw and animalistic. And fucking hot.

I never thought about sex and relationships in that way before. The idea seemed to bubble up from somewhere deeply subconscious.

"Ready to head back?" Connor kissed my neck, seemingly oblivious to the sudden rush of need that overtook me.

I answered by sealing my lips over his, opening wide and surging my tongue into his mouth.

He grinned when our long, passionate kiss ended. "I'll take that as a yes."

We stood from the table together and I caught his grimace before he could hide it.

"What's wrong?" I demanded.

"Nothin'," he said gruffly. "Legs are just sore from being on them all day. I can't wait to take these damn things off." He grabbed a gratuitous handful of my ass. "And take other things off."

"Did you lotion your, um…"

"My stumps?" he laughed. "It's okay, babe, you can say it. And no, I forgot."

"Do it right when you take them off," I insisted. "I don't want you hurting."

"Yes, ma'am," he teased, kissing my temple as he threw a heavy arm around my shoulders.

Thankfully, it was a short walk to the trailer. But just as we got home, we ran into Nigel, the carnival manager.

"Go ahead, babe. I'll catch up." Connor released me. "I'm going to check in with Nigel real quick about our schedule."

"Not too long," I warned him. I knew the longer he stood, the more pain he would be in.

"It'll just be a second." He dropped a quick kiss to my lips before he jogged away. "Start a campfire for us? Just like I showed you."

Grumbling, I went inside and rummaged around for the lighter and kindling. The shitty plastic lighter was nearly out of fluid and we had a hell of a time starting the fire last night, even with Connor's Marine corps survival skills.

On top of that, our kindling was nearly gone.

I gathered up as many dried pine needles and small twigs as I could see in the quickly fading light and proceeded to build the fire.

"Come on, you stupid motherfucker," I cursed as the lighter sparked uselessly until my thumb was sore. The pine needles released smoke but ignited no flames. I blew gently, like Connor showed me whenever they caught a spark, but it would die before catching anything.

"Son of a bitch." I sat back on my heels, frustrated.

"Need some help?"

The dark ink covering his body made him nearly invisible in the fading light. His smile and pale gray eyes were the brightest parts of him, almost looking like they were floating and not attached to a body.

"Don't worry. I'll leave you be," Razvan laughed as he

approached me on long, graceful legs. "But I could help you with that fire."

I shrugged, not wanting to give the impression that I was open to conversation. Where the fuck was Connor?

Razvan kneeled, balancing lightly on the balls of his feet, and grinned at me from across my haphazard arrangement of logs.

"Want to see a magic trick?"

I shrugged again, looking as bored as possible, but I was secretly intrigued.

Razvan cupped a tattooed hand around his mouth and whispered, *"Abra cadabra."*

A single flame shot from his mouth and engulfed the logs and kindling in one fell swoop.

I fell backward on my butt, stunned and scared shitless. One second there was nothing, and then *boom*, fire. From his fucking *mouth*?!

I stared through the flames at his face, calm but with a playful gleam in his eye. What the fuck kind of magic trick was that? His hands were empty, weren't they?

Razvan rose to his feet and gave me a curt, but polite nod as he turned to walk away.

"Enjoy your campfire, miss Melody."

3

MELODY

A beautiful pale man came to me in my dreams.

Sharp, golden eyes watched me, and silky platinum hair fell past his shoulders. His torso was covered in long, lean muscles, his pale skin making him look carved from marble.

Why did he look so familiar to me?

"I miss you," he said in a pained voice, barely above a whisper. "Every day, Roo and Rinna still ask where you are. They need their mother."

He looked at me with those sad golden eyes as he spoke, but it seemed more like he talked to himself. I felt like I was intruding on a private moment, but couldn't break away from his gaze.

"I lost the pack," he continued. "I've searched for days and can't pick up their scent. If they're no longer here, I hope they're running with you, my love."

His sadness made my heart crack into a million pieces. I felt his grief and despair as if it were my own. But why was I here? This was not my place. I wasn't meant to be hearing these things.

"It's just the three of us now," he said. "They're getting bigger and stronger every day since we got away. You'd be so proud."

Out of nowhere, his expression changed. His handsome face went from mournful to grinning. The change was jolting. His grin turned to laughter as his body leaned forward, falling to his hands and knees.

He opened his mouth to reveal a long, forked tongue, and large, scaly wings erupted from his back. I wanted to scream and back away but couldn't move. On all fours he crawled towards me, his body moving from side to side like a reptile.

BANG! BANG! BANG!

"What the fuck!"

I jolted out of my dream, sitting straight up and panting. My heart crashed against my ribs as if desperate to jump out. Next to me, Connor nearly fell out of the bed.

"Whoa! What's wrong?" he looked at me with concern as he maintained his balance.

"Bad dream," I panted, pressing my hand to my chest. The image of that man with wings and a forked tongue crawling toward me burned in my mind.

BANG! BANG! BANG!

I jumped and shrieked, then found myself pressed into Connor's chest.

"It's alright, babe. Just someone at the door," he murmured into my hair, then yelled to the person outside, "hold on a fuckin' minute!"

I curled into a ball against his solid chest while he gently rocked me and rubbed my back. Slowly I felt myself calming, but didn't want to lose the security of his arms. I curled up tighter, pressing against his warm skin.

"Must've been a hell of a dream," he observed. "You look like I did the night of the fireworks."

"It felt so real," I said, my voice shaky. I rubbed my eyes and deepened my breaths, trying to stay solidly here in the waking world.

"Dreaming about the wolves again?"

"No. Kinda. Fuck, I dunno." I leaned my forehead against his shoulder. "I'm losing my damn mind."

I didn't even tell him what happened last night with Razvan and the fire. It couldn't have been real. Whatever he did was just some trick to show off again. He was a good illusionist. I'd give him that much.

"No, you're not." He kissed my forehead and moved my hair out of my face. "A lot of crazy shit happened that night. Your brain is still processing through it."

"Connor!" A voice yelled from the outside. "We need to talk! Shit's changed since last night and I'm fucked."

I recognized the voice as Nigel, the carnival manager. He sounded panicked.

"I told you, one minute!" Connor yelled back. "You okay to get decent, babe? I gotta see what he wants."

I nodded and reluctantly pulled away from his warmth and solidness, looking on the floor for my bra and shorts.

"Let him in for me, babe." Connor pulled a shirt on as he sat on the edge of the bed, his knees hanging over slightly.

"Are you sure?" I tugged my clothing into place, eyeballing his prosthetics leaning against the wall next to him. Back in Drowningville, he had been extremely secretive about his disability, always hiding his prosthetics under long pants.

"It's alright. He knows," he answered softly. "Nigel's an army vet. He gets it."

I nodded and went to the door, pulling it open with a smile.

"Morning, ma'am," he said tersely. He looked like he barely slept. "Is Stilts decent yet?"

It took a moment for Connor's stage name to register in my still-rattled brain.

"Oh, yes! Sorry, come in."

I stepped aside to let him through the narrow door. Connor had lifted himself into one of the chairs at the small table and gestured to the other one for Nigel.

"Mornin' Nigel. What can I do for ya?" His voice was still low, gravelly, and sexy from sleep.

"I'm fucked, Stilts." Nigel sat down heavily at the table.

"Um, should I start some coffee?" I asked, feeling awkward. There was nowhere for me to really go to give them privacy.

"Coffee?" Nigel scoffed. "You got any whiskey in here? 'Cause that's what I fuckin' need."

"Coffee would be great, babe." Connor squeezed my hand before turning to the distraught man. "What's going on?"

"All but six of my fuckin' acts quit on me this mornin," he spat. "That six includes you two."

No way. I nearly dropped the coffeepot. He *had* to be exaggerating.

"What the hell?" Connor echoed my thoughts.

"You heard me right," Nigel said. "Apparently there's auditions for some big Vegas show nearby here. Everyone and their mother went off to chase the big bucks and I'm left with random freaks and shit. No offense."

"None taken." Connor narrowed his eyes at him. "Is this audition for real?"

"Probably not," Nigel spat. "Most likely Arch or one of my other competitors trying to poach my talent, fuckin' snake bastards. What the hell am I gonna do now, Stilts? Tickets are almost sold out! People fuckin' take road trips across the country for this!"

"You still got the Renaissance vendors out here, right?" Connor rubbed his chin thoughtfully.

"Yeah, thank fuckin' God. All the ride and game staff, too. What we don't have is a cohesive show, which is the main fuckin' event! Even my ringmaster up and left!"

"That sucks, man," Connor said sympathetically. "Thanks, babe." He accepted the steaming hot cup of coffee from me.

"Damn right, it sucks," Nigel lamented. "If I have to refund all these tickets, I'll be fuckin' ruined."

"Seems to me the only thing you can do," Connor rubbed his jaw, "is get everyone together to make a single, cohesive show. Make a program and put everybody up on the main stage."

"I dunno, man." Nigel rubbed the back of his neck. "Have you seen some of these weirdos? Covered in tattoos and all their freaky body mods and shit? I don't think that's what this crowd is looking for."

"They're coming here to see weird shit," Connor pointed out. "This isn't some high-class bougie Cirque du Soleil shit you're putting on. This is a backwoods, rinky dink traveling carnival. People are coming for the freaks and the weirdos."

Nigel sighed and shook his head. "That might be the only way, but I know we're gonna have some pearl clutchers, man. I guess partial refunds are better than all refunds."

Connor reached across the table and slapped his shoulder in that encouraging, manly way.

"Come on, man. Where's that army spirit? You've put together a bunch of sad sacks into cohesive units before. Just think of this as a training exercise, sergeant."

Nigel gave a slight nod and stood from the table. "I got my mortgage riding on this shit, Stilts. I can't afford to lose." He looked between both of us. "Meet me at the tavern in a half hour. We're getting all you sideshow people together."

He abruptly left, leaving Connor and me in contemplative silence.

"Sounds serious," I mused, taking a sip of coffee.

"Mm-hm," Connor agreed. "He's an alright dude, despite the shady nature of this business. If we can help him out, I'm all for it."

"You gave him quite the pep talk." I reached over and massaged his shoulder. The muscles were tight, and he groaned as I worked into the knot.

"Seems to be what I'm good at," he chuckled, leaning into my touch.

Dare I say it?

I leaned down and brushed my lips across the shell of his ear. "That's not the only thing you're good at."

"Mm, babe," he moaned, wrapping a large arm around my waist and pulling me into his lap. "How much time do we have again?"

"Half-hour, right?" I straddled his tapered waist and bit gently on his earlobe, knowing how much he liked that.

"Well, you caught me without my legs on." His large hands glided across my thighs as he nipped the skin between my neck and shoulder. "So unless you want to move, we're staying right here."

"Here is exactly where I want you," I whispered back.

A HALF-HOUR LATER, we sat in the same spot in the bar as we did the other night. I brought my coffee mug with me, drinking it down quickly as the other performers filed in. My mind felt soft and fuzzy after messing around with Connor, but I wanted it to be sharp for this meeting.

He stood next to Nigel at the bar, talking to him and another man in low voices. Nigel and the other guy looked just as stressed and frazzled as we saw in our trailer that morning. Connor was the only one who looked alert yet calm. His arms crossed over his chest as his eyes swept between the two other men, mostly listening while they talked.

I drank him in unashamedly, remembering his skillful hands on me just moments ago. Like always, the orgasm he gave me was delicious and satisfying. A sweet release after a perfect amount of teasing and build up.

Still, my thighs rubbed together under the table. An ache for more echoed through me like a drum. He would only touch my clit, nothing more. With every attempt I made to move things further, he stopped. He wouldn't even let me touch him the same way.

I had a feeling I knew why. He wanted to prove that he

respected me and wouldn't take advantage. What Syko did to me at the last carnival left me skittish and even more distrusting of men in general than I already was. But since then, Connor and I slept multiple nights in the same bed with nothing going on.

I *did* trust him, maybe more than he trusted himself.

And I was also a living, breathing woman with physical needs. And I was falling for him.

The lump in my throat wouldn't go away as that thought took hold of my mind.

It didn't matter to me what limbs he was missing or what trauma he faced. There he stood, calm and capable while the men surrounding him, who didn't face nearly the hardships that he did, freaked out like children.

Foreign words and musical laughter floating from the doorway drew my attention away from Connor. My nails dug into my palms at the now-familiar smile and dark, tattooed form of Razvan.

He looked like some kind of biker with dark pants, laced-up combat boots and a matching leather vest with no shirt underneath. Silver rings glittered across his knuckles, as if his long, tattooed fingers needed any more decoration.

Every time I saw him, I seemed to notice another detail, like he was a mystery I was uncovering piece by piece. This time it was the nude woman on his shoulder, drawn in a pinup style with a huge snake wrapping around her body in a way that barely covered her breasts and crotch.

Several of my mom's boyfriends had similar naked lady tattoos, so I usually associated them with trashiness. But on Razvan, it somehow seemed more artistic and tasteful.

He covered his entire body in art and it seemed to fit his style and overall aesthetic.

A sudden flash of my dream appeared in my mind as I studied the tattoo. Something about how the snake was drawn reminded me of how the pale man crawled toward me, whipping back and forth like a reptile.

I looked at him too long and he noticed, flashing me a smile and a wink. Embarrassed, I looked back down at my coffee. He chuckled and said something to one of his friends, but thankfully didn't come over to talk.

Connor finally came back to sit beside me. His face was expressionless, but I knew how hyper-aware of his surroundings he was. He definitely saw me staring at Razvan.

He squeezed my knee as he dropped beside me and kissed my temple as if nothing was amiss. Conflicted, I just wrapped my hands tighter around my mug. I didn't want him to be right. I didn't *want* to want anyone else. Razvan was attractive in that bad-boy kind of way and he obviously knew it.

He's nice to look at, but he's not my type, I thought.

Who was I kidding? I had so little actual dating experience, I couldn't even pinpoint what *was* my type.

Nigel stepped out into the center of the room and all the side conversations died down as everyone turned their attention to him.

"As y'all know, y'all are all that's left of the performers of this show," he began. "With all the other dicks fucking us over, there's too many empty holes in the schedule now. I asked y'all here because we need to combine all y'alls acts into a single show."

He gave a slight nod to Connor, who returned the gesture.

"So all sideshow performers will be shifted to the main stage," Nigel continued. "It'll be a bigger stage and audience than some of you have ever done, which could be great for some of y'alls careers."

A low *whoop-dee-doo* type whistle sounded from Razvan's corner of the room. I'd never heard a whistle sound so defeatist and sarcastic. The man himself sat reclined in a chair, his long, leather-clad legs stretched out in front of him. His arms folded across his chest, fingertips resting on the woman and snake on his arm.

Nigel's jaw clenched at the sound, but chose to ignore him.

"I'd ask some of y'all to, uh, clean up your acts for this audience but I have a feeling that won't go over well." He glared directly at Razvan, who pursed his lips in a mocking kiss. "So you're welcome to put on what y'all have been practicing. We just gotta change the schedule and make everything flow together seamlessly. Oh, and I need a ringmaster to get the crowd amped up and make announcements. Any volunteers?"

The room fell silent for a few moments until Razvan raised his hand high like he was in a classroom.

"Not you, Raz," Nigel glowered. "Don't need you setting attendees on fire and having orgies up on stage."

"On the contrary. That's exactly what you need," the tattooed man answered with a smile.

His friends all guffawed with laughter at that, making crude hand gestures and joking animatedly in their native language.

"I need someone who can look presentable," Nigel

said, turning to face everyone else in the room. "Someone with charisma and charm, who can dazzle a crowd with just a smile."

"Psst!" I poked Connor playfully on the arm and giggled when he lifted an eyebrow and gave me a very skeptical side-eye.

Nigel whipped around and his eyes landed on me, registering for a moment before a massive smile broke out on his face.

"Yes!" he cried jubilantly, raising his fists in the air.

"Huh?" I blinked. "Oh yeah, I was just telling Connor he should do it."

"No, not Connor,." He came forward, leaning across the table, and clasped my hands in his. "You, my dear."

4

MELODY

I laughed, certain he was joking, but his watery eyes bore into mine like I was the last woman on earth.

"Yes, you would be perfect!" he declared, then looked sheepish. "Erm, what's your name, again, hun?"

"Melody," I snapped, yanking my hands out of his grip. "And hell no, I'm not doing it! I'm part of Connor's act."

"Connor can be solo like how he's always done before." Nigel looked at him with a plea in his eyes. "Help me out here, man."

Connor rested his elbows on the table, propping his chin up in his hands as he looked deep in thought. I could practically see his brain working, going through all the possible outcomes. That alone started to make me panic.

"Connor," I demanded. "You're not seriously considering this?"

He lifted his chin off his hands and looked over at me. "I think you'd be good at it, babe."

"Yes!" Nigel cried with relief. "You're the only one here with any sense of class, miss Melody. None of these crusty folks know how to walk or speak with any kind of elegance."

I stared at him, open-mouthed and dumbfounded. *Me*, elegant and classy? Had he even looked at me?

"You do know how to capture a crowd," Connor added softly.

"She already has," Razvan said from across the room. Great. Now I realized everyone was staring at me.

"Y'all can't be serious," I protested. "I'm as trashy as they come."

"Don't say that," Connor scolded. "It doesn't matter where you're from. He's right. You have a natural ability to dazzle a crowd. I've seen you do it without even saying a word."

I remembered the rush and thrill of our first night performing together. The audience was captivated. I had no doubt we showed everyone up, and we were the first act of the night.

Even with Syko before he assaulted me, I felt a bit of that rush after I got over the nervousness. The truth was, I *liked* putting on a show and being a character. The energy from the audience was addictive like a drug, and I wanted to entertain more and more to feed off that energy.

But still, *ringmaster*? Surely that was a job for seasoned performers?

"I'm flattered, Nigel," I said, forcing a smile. "Really, I am. But I've literally been onstage twice in my life, both in the past week. I barely have enough experience in my own act, let alone leading an entire show."

"It's as good a time as any to learn." He winked at me, but then frowned when I didn't look convinced. To everyone's surprise, he fell to his knees and placed his hands in my lap. "Please, Melanie—"

"Melody," Connor and I corrected him in unison.

"Melody, my first grandchild is about to be born. I got a mortgage I'm already underwater on. If this show isn't a success, I lose *everything*." He clasped my hands again, looking up at me desperately. "Please, sweetheart. You're my one chance at this."

Damn it. It was like he knew I had a soft spot for others in need. Now I had to worry about him and his family suffering.

I looked over at Connor, who shrugged, but a smile twitched on his lips.

"You'd be great at it, babe. But it's completely up to you."

Silence fell heavily around the bar as everyone waited for my decision. I took a deep breath and released it.

"Okay, I guess."

Nigel whooped victoriously and stood to wrap me in a bone-crushing hug.

"Thank you, thank you, thank you."

"Alright, let her go," Connor growled possessively.

"Oh, dear sweet Jesus." Nigel wiped either tears or sweat from his face. "I can't thank you enough for this, Melody. You're seriously saving my ass here."

"Sure, but like," I didn't even know what questions to ask, "What do I *do*? I have to learn some stuff, right?"

"Yes, yes, of course." Nigel pulled himself together and resumed his business-like demeanor again. "You'll want to meet everyone. Get to know everyone's acts so you can entice the crowd as you announce them. Think of it like a sales pitch."

"Okay," I said blankly. I'd never sold a thing in my life before. Except drinks at the bar, and I didn't exactly need a sales pitch for that.

"We will all help you," Razvan hollered from across the room. He winked and bit his lip suggestively as he spread his legs wide. My whole body heated as if he lit me like a match. Did I *really* want to know what he wanted to help me with?

"Yes, they'll tell you what to say," Nigel agreed, apparently missing the innuendo. "Based on their strengths and how they've been announced at past performances before."

He stood and gestured to the other man he'd been talking to with Connor. "This is Herman, my event coordinator and marketing director. He'll be talking to you all about scheduling and transitioning between acts. Once that's settled, we all come together tomorrow to rehearse."

Connor groaned, and he wasn't the only one. People preferred rehearsing in private, or with their own clique of people.

Nigel ignored the grumbles and waved his hands to dismiss us. "Y'all can go back to your business for now."

Chairs scraped back against the wood floor as everyone stood and filed out the door. I remained sitting, wanting to leave last as I stared at my now-cold coffee in front of me. What the hell had I gotten myself into?

"Come on, babe." Connor ushered me up and I reluctantly followed.

Razvan and his crew approached the door just as we did. We paused to let them through, but in a flash of leather and metal, the tattooed man waved us through.

"After you, please. I insist," he smirked. I couldn't tell if he was being genuine or mocking us.

Once outside I heard a low, smooth whisper behind me say, "I never miss a chance to admire such a lovely rear view."

I froze in my tracks, my whole body burning with either desire or fury. With everywhere my mind and instincts were in that moment, it was impossible to tell which. I decided to go with fury.

After letting Syko get away with what he did, no man would disrespect me again and expect to live it down.

I turned around, snapping my head in the direction of that playful grin and steely gray eyes.

"Don't you ever talk to me like that again." I fought to keep my voice from shaking.

Razvan's eyes widened, more in amusement than surprise. My whole body quivered like a bowl of jello, but I set my jaw and clenched my fists, determined not to crumble.

"I like a woman with fire," he said huskily. "But don't worry, I'll honor your request." His grin widened like a Cheshire cat. "I'll speak to you in Romanian instead if you'd prefer that." He let out a string of beautiful, flowing sounds which sent his friends doubling over with laughter. From the mischievous look in his eye, I had no doubt whatever he said was far worse than what I reprimanded him for.

Without another word, I turned and stalked away with Connor back to our trailer. I had enough on my plate now without some foul-mouthed, tattooed pervert creeping into my thoughts.

"Damn, babe," Connor chuckled, rubbing the nape of my neck. "A little harsh, don't you think?"

In spite of how good his hands felt, I pulled away and looked at him with a stunned expression.

"Don't tell me you're defending him talking to me like that?" I felt wounded, like he wasn't on my side after all.

"He was giving you a compliment." His hand snaked around my waist and down to my hip. "And he was right. This is a very nice rear view."

I pulled away from him again, the disgust apparent on my face. "I can't believe it. Not you, too."

"What? It might've not been the romantic compliment, but give the guy a break. It's his second language."

"That's not what it was and you know it," I snapped. "He knew exactly what he was saying. It was gross and inappropriate."

"Okay, so he's rough around the edges. But you can tell that just by looking at him. He's probably lived in a caravan or whatever his whole life. You can't expect him to compare thee to a summer's day or whatever the fuck."

"Why are you so dead set on making excuses for him?" I sat in front of our campfire, pouting. But the glowing embers just reminded me of Razvan's fire trick, which only fucked with my mind even more.

"Because of what I told you earlier, babe. Guys are gonna be attracted to you. They're gonna make their interest known in different ways. Some more tactful than others. That guy didn't mean you any harm, babe. He's not a Syko."

"How do you know that? We don't know him."

"I can read people pretty well and I think you can, too. Sure, he wants to take you to bed, but he won't touch you without permission. He won't hurt you. Even if he wanted to, he knows he'd have to go through me."

I looked up at him, sitting across the fire from me with his forearms on his knees and green eyes gazing intently into mine. My soldier, my protector. Those eyes never missed anything, whether it was in our surroundings or the emotion on my face.

"You're gonna have to get to know him anyway, as the new ringmistress," he added softly.

"He did... something the other night," I whispered like a confession.

Connor's eyes narrowed, and the muscles in his shoulders flexed with tension. Just those small indicators of his fierce protection made me want to crawl into his lap and ride him.

"What did he do, Mel?"

"I couldn't get the fire started and he..." I raked my fingers through the tangles in my hair, completely unsure how to describe it. "It looked like he lit the fire by blowing on it. Not like how you showed me but like he *breathed* fire."

Connor relaxed, a lopsided smirk emerging on his face. "I'm sure fire breathing is part of his act, babe. He was just showing off for you."

"I know it had to be a trick, but he didn't have a torch or fluid or anything." I was rambling now as the scene played over and over in my head. I saw every detail like a photograph and could not find a way to explain it.

"He's a professional. He knows how to hide his shit." Connor's smile dropped. "Did it scare you, babe?"

"A little," I admitted, curling up in my seat.

Like he said, I didn't think Razvan would hurt me. I didn't get a feeling of danger or discomfort around him. No, what really scared me was how drawn I felt to him.

The fire thing didn't seem like an ordinary magic trick, but something unexplainable and otherworldly. In a lot of ways, he had a similar effect on me as the wolf man.

I was curious about him but my curiosity got me in trouble before. It made me throw caution to the wind and now that I had Connor, it put him at risk too.

"I'm going for a walk," I muttered, rising to my feet.

"Runnin' away, are ya?" he called after me, but I heard the laughter in the voice. He knew I'd come back, no matter how much I wanted to dive under his blankets and hide.

I also had half a mind to look over my shoulder, to entice him to chase me. We could find some private place away from here. Maybe a meadow full of soft grass that miraculously didn't also have a ton of bugs. We'd lay down there and I wouldn't just tell him, I'd *show* him how much he meant to me. How it was *him* I craved and no one else.

But I shoved my clenched hands in my pockets and kept walking.

A barely-marked walking trail made a loop around the fairgrounds so I walked that to clear my head. I was close enough to still see the Ferris wheel but far enough away from people that I'd be left alone.

After a couple of laps around the grounds, I started to warm up to the idea of becoming ringmistress. The role didn't require *that* much talking. The main aspect seemed to be exuding confidence and charisma. Traits that I didn't have but could probably fake well enough.

I was starting to look forward to returning to camp and getting to know the other acts. Unlike in Drowningville, no one seemed openly hostile or predatory toward me. The few other women here, the burlesque dancers and acrobats, seemed indifferent toward me, which was fine.

At this point, I wasn't expecting to make friends. Being with Connor like this was certainly the last thing I expected.

I chewed my lip as I completed my final loop and started heading back. He didn't want to be my boyfriend and while I kind of understood his reasons, hearing it still stung.

A snapping of twigs made me stop in my tracks. My breath froze in my lungs. It definitely wasn't me.

"Is someone there?" I called.

Thick brush and trees grew close to the edge of the trail. With the fairgrounds set up like a miniature village, I forgot how deep in the wild woods we were.

Another snap and a flash of white. I spun around, then nearly fell to my knees.

A man stood there, pale and beautiful, with golden eyes. Silvery-platinum hair fell past his shoulders. He watched me with an expression I couldn't read.

My throat felt like it was closing up. My heart was moments away from crashing out of my chest. I'd never been more afraid in my life, not even when Syko had me trapped onstage.

This was the man from my dreams. Was he going to sprout those wings and crawl toward me in that reptilian way?

I wanted to run with every cell in my body, but my legs refused to obey.

"Mel, babe!"

I looked ahead, Connor's voice pulling me out of my

stupor. He was jogging toward me, his face looking pained as each step put pressure on his legs.

"Babe, you okay?" His eyes, green as the forest surrounding us, searched through mine with concern.

"I saw..." How could I even begin to describe it?

I turned to look where he'd been standing, and the pale man was gone.

RAZVAN

"Ooh, what does this one mean?" the blonde giggled, tracing the dark lines inside my forearm. I had forgotten her name. Sasha? Lara? Something like that.

"It means nothing," I told her honestly. "I got that done while I was drunk in Paris. Or maybe it was in Rio, I can't remember."

The girls tittered and giggled as if that was the funniest thing I'd ever said. Last night I took the blonde and her brunette friend to bed. Don't get me wrong, it was a fun night, but by mid-morning, I was tired of them.

I already finished my morning knife practice before Nigel called us all to that meeting, so I had little to do for the rest of the day. Besides, it was just so hard to get away from all the lovely burlesque girls when they fawned all over me and wanted to know the meanings of my tattoos. I'd challenge any man to pull himself away from that.

"Can I see your tongue again?" the voluptuous brunette

asked me, leaning close. She was definitely Annie. No, maybe Angela. Fuck me.

I smiled and obliged, sticking my forked tongue out and wiggled both sides of it independently. She enjoyed that immensely on her clit last night while I pounded the fuck out of her blonde friend.

My tongue wasn't naturally that way. Contrary to popular belief about dragon shifters, we had normal tongues in human form. I had it intentionally split on a whim one day. My tattoo artist back in Romania knew a guy who did more extreme body modifications, and he happened to be in town that day. It hurt like a bitch for a second, but my fast healing abilities took the edge off pretty quickly.

The brunette cooed and giggled, bringing a soft hand to my face as she leaned even closer. She closed her eyes and tilted her face as her lips parted. Internally, I groaned but gave her a quick kiss with a tongue caress, like she wanted. This girl was already getting all starry-eyed with me and I could see her becoming a stage-5 clinger.

"Um, should I come back later?"

All three of our heads turned to see the new ring-mistress, Melody, standing awkwardly at the edge of the burlesque dancers' camp.

Melody. Now *that* was a name I could not forget.

"Yeah, probably." The brunette snaked a hand inside my leather cut to stroke my bare chest. "We're a little busy."

She licked my ear, and I jumped. Fuck, I already told her I hated that shit.

"Actually, no." I forcibly removed her hand from me and moved away. "Now's the perfect time, miss Melody."

Her blush was adorable, but her chin lifted defiantly, and her eyes narrowed at me. Ah, so she was still unhappy about me complimenting her backside earlier.

"I was hoping to talk to the burlesque troupe about their act," she said. "I'll come around the camp and talk to your people later."

"Why not hit two birds with one stone?" I flashed her my most charming smile. "I lead the Flaming Swords. Anything you want to know about our act, you are welcome to ask me."

She shifted uncomfortably on her feet. My suggestion made sense but she was still uneasy about me. I couldn't blame her. She seemed skittish, like a feral kitten backed into a corner. The only man she seemed to trust was Connor, with how she remained attached to his hip.

"Hi, I'm Lana." Ah, that was her name. The blonde stood to greet Melody with a friendly smile and hand-shake. She was definitely the most down-to-earth one. "We're the Southern Belles burlesque troupe. Congratulations on becoming Ringmistress!"

"Thanks," Melody said shyly. "It's nice to meet you. I still have no idea what the hell I'm doing."

"Aw, you'll be great!" Lana waved her hand toward the folding chairs and fallen logs around their campfire. "Join us for some tea and a bite?"

"Sure, thank you." Melody gave her a smile and sat a bit off to the side of me, probably so she wouldn't have to look at me directly.

Meanwhile, Lana's brunette friend had all but climbed into my lap, shooting dirty looks at Melody the entire time.

"Let me up for a bit, hon." I patted the side of her hip. "My legs are falling asleep."

She let out an annoying whine and wrapped her arms tighter around my neck, nuzzling her face into my chest, and began kissing me there. I saw Melody look away, and I glanced over pleadingly at Lana.

"Oh, get off him already, Ally," she chided her friend jokingly. "Let the man breathe."

Ally reluctantly slumped off me, but not before pressing her mouth to mine and jamming her tongue between my lips. I didn't return it and pulled away. This girl's possessiveness was already starting to piss me off.

No one possessed me. Especially not a woman.

But Melody? She intrigued me.

She made my dragon restless, unlike any other woman before. The moment I first saw her, I wanted to do more than just show off my knife skills. The beast within me wanted to beat its scaled wings, roar loud enough to shatter these humans' eardrums, and set the entire forest ablaze just to show he was a worthy mate.

Humans pushed their animal instincts so far back into their psyche, but we shifters, or *mutaţie* as my people called them, fought a daily battle of instinct and personhood.

Still, I kept my distance as Melody settled in, accepting a mug of tea from Lana as they chatted. It would do me no good to come onto her strongly. I had to treat her carefully, just like the skittish kitten she was.

Ally settled next to me, still pressing her leg against my thigh. Still too close for comfort, but at least she was no longer in my lap. Nothing made my dick softer than blatant desperation.

I watched Melody with interest as she slowly grew more relaxed in my presence. Just like her name, her voice was musical when she talked. Nigel made the right choice in her as ringmistress. She would seduce the audience with that face and voice, even if she didn't have the confidence to believe it yet.

Despite the effect she had on my dragon, she didn't smell like a shifter. On that note, she didn't smell entirely human either. It was all I could do not to lean closer and smell that rich, ebony black hair up close.

"Why don't we go back in the tent?" Ally squeezed my thigh and tried to give me a seductive look. "Let them talk business."

"This business concerns me, too," I snarled, ripping her hand off me. "And as lovely as you are, hon, desperation is not a good look. You'd do well to remember that."

Her mouth formed an O of surprise and she finally scooted away, blinking back tears. I didn't enjoy making women cry, but it was the only way to get through to her. I had been willing to fuck her again, but now I was doubting that. From what experience taught me, she'd start talking about weddings and babies the next morning. No, thank you.

Melody finally turned those large, chocolate brown eyes on me, and my dragon startled. It was all I could do to keep excited puffs of smoke coming from my nostrils. The little fire trick from last night was risky to show her, and quite possibly an unwise move. I still wasn't sure *why* I did it, aside from the scaly beast inside dying to impress her. I hadn't met anyone in years who knew I wasn't fully human.

"So tell me about what you do, Razvan," she inquired

shyly. Her eyes met mine for a moment and then darted away.

"So glad you asked," I grinned. "My crew and I are quite multi-talented when it comes to fire and sharp metal things. We do the usual knife throwing and juggling, sword-swallowing, but we add a little pyromania to it, too. One of our best acts is having a sword fight with flaming blades."

"It's a really cool show!" Lana piped up. "Kind of scary, too."

"The crowd loves a little danger," I said with a wink.

Melody chewed her lip. "Do you ever have people stand in front of a dartboard which you throw knives at?"

I tilted my head. It was an oddly specific question. "We used to with people from the audience, but not so much anymore. We've never had any unfortunate accidents but too many others have and the carnivals got sued. Now most managers forbid it to cover their own asses."

"You did it with audience members?" Her eyes widened.

"Yeah, it added a little bit of reality to the show," I shrugged. "Totally harmless as long as it's done correctly. But some dumb fucks ruined it for everyone."

Melody nodded as she mulled over what I told her. She looked especially adorable when deep in thought. I wondered if she originated from my country. With her dark eyes, dark hair, and pale skin, she had that lovely gothic look that Romanian women were known for. A look that I was a sucker for after being in the States these past few years. These cheery southern belles, while bright, beautiful, and charming, I quickly found were not my type.

"Anything else you'd like to tell me?" Melody asked.

"Absolutely." I leaned forward, those deep chocolate eyes consuming me. "Perhaps over a drink?"

I half expected her to recoil from me as if in disgust, but she didn't. Her slender eyebrows raised, but she held my gaze coolly.

"Thank you Razvan, but I'm not a drinker," she answered.

"Call me Raz." I grinned, not willing to give up. "How about over dinner, then?"

"I have plans."

Of course she did. With her man, no doubt. Anyone with eyes could tell they were together, but I had senses that were beyond human. I could smell Connor's desire for her and hers for him, but I didn't get the sense that he wanted to claim her as off limits. When I approached her in the bar, his lack of reaction confirmed it loud and clear.

He was *hers,* but he didn't demonstrate that she was *his*.

For some reason, despite his feelings, he didn't feel worthy of her. Their relationship was intriguing, although not as intriguing as the woman herself sitting before me.

Melody was harder to read than Connor. She acted completely human, but there was something else there. I couldn't decipher her desires as easily. Maybe because of how young she was, she didn't know them entirely herself.

As much as she fascinated me, she was also blatantly rejecting me, and I was not one to push a woman past her boundaries.

I lowered my eyes and smiled, accepting her refusals as gracefully as I could. There was a difference between persistence and pestering, and I did not want to find myself in the latter category.

"How about we go for a walk?"

My eyes snapped up, unable to hide my surprise.

"You want to walk with *me*?" I asked in disbelief.

She nodded, the adorable blush rising in her cheeks. "It'll be easiest for us to talk, don't you think?"

I smiled. This girl was full of surprises. "Definitely. When would you like to go?"

"How about now?"

My dragon yearned to roar and beat his wings in victory, but I kept a cool exterior. It seemed the skittish little kitten wasn't so afraid after all.

I stood from my seat, ignoring Ally's look of jealousy, and held my hand out toward the nearby walking path.

"Shall we?"

Melody rose as well, following my lead and keeping a comfortable distance between us. That was fine with me. Being alone with her was more than I could hope for at that moment.

We walked side-by-side in silence on the first part of the trail. She chewed her lip and kept her hands clasped in front of her body. She seemed like she wanted to ask me something but couldn't spit it out.

"I would ask why you wanted to be alone with me, but I'm worried about getting another reaction like this morning," I teased, testing the waters.

She humored me with a small smile. "I might have overreacted to that. Sorry for biting your head off."

"Nothing to fear. As you can see, my head is still firmly attached."

She gave me a light, musical laugh that time. "It's an expression."

"I know. I'm just playing the adorable, clueless foreigner," I said with a wink.

"Where are you from, Raz?" Her use of my shortened name made my heart skip a beat.

"Romania," I answered. "The birthplace of Dracula."

"Really?" Her eyebrows lifted in surprise.

"Yes, Transylvania is a province in my country," I smiled. "A beautiful place actually, miss Melody."

"You can call me Mel," she murmured.

I preferred using her full name, but she was opening up to me now rather than retreating. I wouldn't ruin such a chance.

"So what else is there to your act that you wanted to tell me?" Her tone turned more business-like, but she still had that kitten-like curiosity in her voice.

I stopped walking and turned to look at her. "You want to know how I lit your campfire last night."

She swallowed nervously, but stood squarely and fearlessly in front of me. "So you're saying that wasn't an ordinary magic trick?"

"Depends on what your definition of ordinary is," I countered.

She blinked. "I'm not sure what you're trying to say. But I keep playing it over in my head. I didn't smell lighter fluid. I didn't see a match or anything to ignite a flame."

"And you still thought walking out into the woods alone with me was wise?" I flashed a flirtatious smile in hopes she wouldn't take the question too seriously.

Her fists clenched at her sides. She lowered her chin to glare at me.

"You won't hurt me. I'm not sure how I know that, but you're being evasive now, so I still don't entirely trust you."

Those last words made me bristle defensively, though I tried not to let it show. Of course she didn't trust me. This was our first real conversation together. But I had a knee jerk reaction to that statement because of how much it seemed to follow me everywhere.

People didn't trust me because of how I looked. If not my extensive body mod collection, it was rumors of my sexual escapades or my affinity for fire and sharp blades. Even though I'd never been dishonest, deceitful, or manipulated another person, I gave the implication that I wasn't trustworthy.

Women loved to fuck me, but I never met one that didn't think I would cheat in some way. I was the bad boy fantasy, not the guy they took home to meet their family. Even clingy Ally saw me as a project she could improve, not someone she could take as-is. Not that I wanted to give up my freedom to fuck around as I pleased. It would just be nice if someone could see me differently.

Still, Melody had no idea of my defensiveness around the concept of trust, so I just gave her a tight smile.

"You're right, I won't hurt you," I said. "And I'm not being evasive, just bantering."

Her eyes narrowed, and she opened her mouth to say something, but the energy in the air immediately shifted. My dragon raised his defenses as I tuned into my surroundings. Another shifter was nearby. It felt like the same one I sensed earlier.

Melody's face went white as a sheet as she whipped around. She sensed it, too. Interesting.

And she was scared, but also seemed like she was familiar with this presence.

"Stay by me," I instructed, stepping in front of her and pulling her behind my back.

Her breath came out in soft puffs as her small hands

rested on my shoulders, but I couldn't be distracted by that touch now.

My dragon tasted the air, sniffing out this shy shifter's motivations as Melody and I turned in a cautious circle.

When the feedback returned to me, I smiled and relaxed.

"I just saw a flash of white fur," Melody said in a hushed whisper. "It's not the first time, either. I think it's... well, it's kind of a long story."

My shoulders shook as I laughed. I took one of Melody's hands from my shoulder and turned to face her.

"You have nothing to be afraid of, *steluţa*," I told her. "It seems you have a shy admirer."

❧   6   ❧

MELODY

I blinked up at Razvan's steely gray eyes, though for a moment they seemed to take on a tinge of red. And maybe I imagined it, but I thought I saw his pupils narrow to slits like a reptile.

"An admirer?" I repeated.

"Yes," he confirmed. "He senses your fear and doesn't wish to scare you, so he keeps his distance. But you have my word, *steluţa*, he will not harm you. If anything, he is acting like an unseen bodyguard."

His charming grin spread, almost hiding the small tattoos near the outer corners of his eyes. "You're a lucky woman, having all these admirers looking out for you."

I didn't know what to make of that. Was he including himself in that statement?

"How do you know what... my admirer is feeling?" I asked. "Do you know what it, er, he is?"

The grin faded, his expression turning serious and even intimidating in a sexy way.

"Yes," he answered. "But I'm not sure how much you know or *want* to know."

"I have so many questions," I admitted, my mind swirling with memories of the wolf man and his family. My recent dreams mixed in, almost feeling like memories themselves. "But I'm not sure who's the right person to ask."

"Right, of course. You don't trust me yet." Razvan smirked, but I felt some tension coming off him like he felt defensive about my saying that. "If you show your admirer you're not afraid, maybe he'll approach you himself, *steluța*."

"What's that word you keep calling me?" I demanded. He said it enough times, but I had no idea if it was a pet name or insult.

"Ah, I can't tell you all my secrets now," he said playfully. "I want you to invite me on another walk in the woods."

"Is it something your friends will laugh at if they hear it?" I was still a little on edge about earlier today, but was beginning to see what Connor meant about him. This guy was different. Definitely a character, but nothing about him told my instincts to stay away.

"Not at you, no," he said softly. "But they'll give me a good ribbing for sure."

"That doesn't make any sense to me," I mumbled.

"Maybe it will one day." He winked at me. "You have a lot to do, so I won't take any more of your time, Melody."

I barely realized that we'd been walking back in the direction we came. The forest path gave way to the burlesque camp, open and welcoming with its cozy fire and tents.

I turned to Razvan, suddenly feeling shy, like this was the end of a date.

"Well, thanks for uh, looking out for me." I swallowed. "And telling me about you. Your act, I mean."

"It's been my pleasure," he said with a slight bow of his head. "Until next time, *steluța*."

I turned down my own path to continue my way down to the other campsites, not wanting to leave my eyes lingering on him for long. He and that girl Ally seemed like they were a thing. I definitely didn't want another girl thinking I had my claws sunk into her man.

Curiosity got the better of me as I walked, and I peeked over my shoulder to look back at him. To my surprise, he went right past the burlesque tent and continued on into the woods. Why wouldn't he go right back to the woman fawning over him?

None of your business, Mel, I told myself.

Our walk in the woods left me with more questions than answers, really. I had enough buzz words to use in my ringmistress announcements, but I didn't really learn anything about him at all.

He's probably a vampire. He's from the land of Dracula, after all, I mused.

AN HOUR LATER, I returned to my own camp to find Connor practicing some crazy shit.

He was shirtless near our trailer, wearing long sweatpants covering his legs. His bronze, sun-kissed skin was glossy in a thin sheen of sweat.

He dropped backward into a handstand, kicking his

feet straight up into the air. The pant cuffs cinched tightly around the metal ankle joint, keeping his pant legs from slipping down as he slowly bent and straightened his elbows.

I quickly realized he was doing push-ups with his entire bodyweight. With rigorous control and strength, he lowered himself until he nearly kissed the ground before pushing himself back up with the same fluid movement.

He did that ten times before swinging his feet down and standing right-side up again. His red face looked surprised when he saw me.

"You're back," he stated, sounding just as surprised.

"Yeah, made my rounds." My core flushed with heat as I approached him, drinking in that ripped, tan torso.

Saying nothing, he turned away and picked up a towel to wipe his face and neck.

"Practicing without me?" I teased, leaning against the trailer.

"You're not part of my act anymore, *Ringmistress*."

Maybe he meant to tease me back, but through the towel his voice came out low and gruff. And he still wasn't looking at me. My heart started to feel like it was being squeezed in a fist.

"Hey, is something wrong?" I reached out to put a hand on his arm, and he promptly pulled away.

"No. Why would anything be wrong?"

"Because you're acting like a dick."

His green eyes finally met mine, buried under a furrowed brow and a scowl on that handsome face.

"I just didn't expect you to get back from *making your rounds* so soon."

"So soon? It's been a couple of hours. And why are you

mad that I'm back?"

"I'm not mad." His jaw clenched. "Forget I said anything."

He stormed off, leaving me stunned for a moment before my own anger spurred me to follow him.

"I don't know what crawled up your ass and died, Connor, but don't take your shit out on me!"

He ignored me, taking two long strides into the trailer, and slammed the door after him. I followed, yanking it open and slamming it twice as hard.

"Get out, Mel," he growled, whipping around to face me. With all his muscles coiled and flexed with power, he looked ready to tear the inside of this tiny trailer apart.

"No." I stood my ground, despite the fear creeping into my voice. Fear mixed with arousal, creating an explosive chemical cocktail inside me just from watching his abs flex as he breathed. "You don't get to be an asshole to me for no reason. You owe me an explanation, Connor."

"I don't owe you shit, Melody!" he yelled. "You have everything of mine already!"

"What the fuck does that mean?!" I shouted back.

Tears of frustration burned in my eyes. I hated yelling more than anything, but running and hiding never made it go away. I knew Connor wouldn't hurt me, not physically anyway, but I wasn't going to let him make me feel small and powerless. I was done feeling that way.

He rushed at me so quickly, I thought for a fleeting moment I was wrong about him. Fear and lifelong instincts told me to flinch and look away. I wasn't ready for him to lift me up and press me between his hard body and the wall. I wasn't ready for his lips to come crashing down on mine to consume me.

"Why do you have to do this to me, Mel?" His teeth nipped just below my earlobe, making me cry out and cling to him. He just pressed against me harder with a heavy groan.

"Do what?" I asked in a shaky whisper. A rush of wetness flooded my core so fast. I was so confused, so unbelievably turned on, I thought I was going insane.

"Make me feel this way." Pinning me to the wall with his hips, his large hands enveloped my ribcage. "Make me feel *anything* at all."

"Connor," I gasped, bringing his mouth to mine like he was the air I desperately needed to live.

Our tongues clashed in a fierce battle for dominance. He kneaded my breasts in such a way that was intense, but not painful. I shifted my legs to wrap snugly around his waist and found his erection straining hard against his pants.

"Mel," he groaned, dragging his burning hot mouth down my neck. "I don't deserve you, babe, but you're all I want."

"Stop that." I wrapped my arms around his shoulders, pressing my chest and my core to him. "You deserve so much more than me."

"No, you stop." His voice carried a light chuckle, but was still low and full of need. "I've done awful things, babe. I'm fucking selfish to want you this bad."

"Then be selfish."

I slid a hand down his chest, memorizing every muscle, hair, and scar with my palm until I reached the front of his pants. The outline of his bulge greeted me and I cupped my palm along his thick length. He shivered and moaned as I touched him, then slid his arms around my back to peel me away from the wall.

Like free-falling through the air onstage, I felt weight-less as he carried me until the bed supported my back.

"Connor, will you..." I gasped during the moments my mouth was free from his to speak, "...will you let me touch you this time?"

He paused—his intense, passionate movements becoming slow and methodical.

"You're telling me to be selfish, so who am I to say no?"

I felt his smile against my skin and joy lifted in my heart. Now *I* could stop feeling selfish for a few moments and reciprocate what he gave me.

"Connor." I brushed my lips past his ear. I loved saying his name and from the way he moaned into my neck, I guessed he loved hearing it. "I want all of you."

To prove my point, I slipped a hand inside his pants and boxers. My fingers brushed past his solid, silky head to wrap around his hot shaft. In response, my molten core closed agonizingly around nothing. I needed it, needed *him*.

"Mel." His voice was thick with desire. "You have all of me here." He took my other hand and pressed it to his chest, where his racing heartbeat kissed my palm. "I want you more than anything, but you don't have to settle for *my* body to please you."

"I told you to stop it," I growled, biting down on his ear in frustration until he yelped. "I want *you*, Connor. Touch me, I'm so wet for you."

I directed his hand to the furnace between my legs, instantly sighing from the pressure of his fingers on my slick folds.

He knew me there better than anyone, despite knowing each other for such a short time. He could always tell exactly what I loved, needed, and craved, and teased me relentlessly until I went off like an atomic bomb.

"Connor," I moaned as I rocked against his palm, growing desperate to ease the mounting pressure growing inside me. "You're the only one that's ever pleased me."

He stopped suddenly and pulled away to look at me with a puzzled expression.

"So when you made your rounds earlier, what did you mean?"

I blinked up at him, equally confused. "I talked with everyone about their acts for my ringmistress speech. What did you think I meant?"

He dropped his face on the mattress next to mine. A muffled sound came from his mouth and his body shook with... laughter?

"Connor!" I twisted out from under him to look at him better. "What the hell did you think I did?"

"Fuck. I'm sorry, Mel." He wiped his eyes, and I realized he was crying from laughing so hard. "My mind went somewhere while you were gone and I didn't stop to think about how ridiculous it was."

I stared at him, agape. "You didn't seriously think I slept with the whole carnival, did you?"

"Not the whole carnival, no." He giggled as he tried to compose himself. "I figured you probably got cozy with that Razvan guy, though."

"What?! No! I barely know him!"

"You barely know me," he pointed out.

"I know you a hell of a lot better than him," I huffed. "And anyway, he has a girlfriend or fuck buddy or whatever.

She was all over him at the burlesque camp."

"Something tells me he doesn't really limit himself." Connor smiled wryly.

"It doesn't matter, anyway. Nothing happened." The realization hit me like a ton of bricks. "Is that why you were so pissed off when I came back?"

"Kind of," he sighed. "More pissed at myself, really. I convinced myself you went for him since I told you I'd be fine with it. Then I realized I was jealous of you spending time with him, then pissed off at myself because I have no right to be jealous. And just, yeah. An infinite loop."

"Oh, Connor," I breathed.

I rolled over on top of him and kissed him with every ounce of emotion pouring out of me right then. No words could describe how he made me feel, how desperately I wanted him to see himself as I did.

He cradled my face sweetly as he kissed me back.

"You were right, babe," he whispered against my lips. "I shouldn't have taken it out on you. I'm sorry."

"So, you want to be my boyfriend now?" I nipped playfully at his jaw, but when the answer didn't come, I felt a sinking feeling in my stomach.

"I still don't want you to limit yourself to just me," he sighed. "I just... need to deal with my feelings about it better."

"And I still think you're making this an issue when it doesn't need to be one." I slid my leg across him to straddle his waist. "But we can talk about that later."

Our eyes met for a hot, electric moment before his mouth devoured mine again. This time, nothing stopped us or got us off track.

❧ 7 ❧

MELODY

He tore my shirt and bra off, flinging them both violently across the trailer. I lifted my hips to peel his pants and boxers down, finally revealing his glorious cock. He was hard, thick and mouth watering, and it was just as tanned as the rest of his body.

I finished undressing him, sliding his clothes past his prosthetics and the silicone sleeves that held them in place on his legs. Honestly, I found it hot that part of his body was made of metal. Like he was some kind of bionic man or sexy android. He survived horrors that made him greater than any ordinary man. If only he could see that.

But my main focus was not on his legs, but on *him*. The warmth and skin and scars that told stories and shaped this man who captured my heart, too.

He peeled my shorts and panties off and skimmed his fingertips with slow fascination back up my legs. He touched my ankles, calves, and the backs of my knees before taking a firm grip on my thighs and hips.

I loved how every touch and every kiss of his was

deliberate, confident. His mouth pressed kisses to my belly while he kneaded my flesh. He was roughness, gentleness, and intensity all wrapped into one package and I could not get enough.

My fingers tried to memorize every crevice between his muscles, every vein that pulsed through his skin. How could he not realize how incredibly hot he was? How could he really think I'd want to sleep with some stranger over him? This body needed four men to restrain him in a bar fight. This body put a huge wolf man over its shoulders and carried him to safety. This body made me feel safe, protected, and like a *woman*, not some silly, lovesick girl.

I wrapped my hand around his thick shaft again, pressing hard and hot against my leg.

"Mm," he moaned and thrust into my hand, the velvety skin gliding through my fingers. "Like this, babe."

He covered my hand with his and guided my strokes. I watched his face, fascinated and so incredibly turned on at his lip bites, his accelerated breaths, and his head dropping back in ecstasy.

"Keep doing that and I'll be off in no time," he grinned, gently pulling my hand away and bringing my palm to his lips.

"You got me almost there already," I replied huskily, resuming my position on top of him. His cock pulsed with heat against my sensitive core, my clit tingling from the hard pressure. My blood felt like liquid fire in my veins. I felt like I wanted this forever. I never knew how much I needed him.

"Hang on, babe." Connor reached above us to fumble through a shelf just above the bed. I took the opportunity to run my hands down his perfect chest and abs again.

Fuck, I could hardly believe I was in bed with this sexy beast of a man.

He produced a square foil wrapper and tore it open. "Never thought I'd be using these again."

"Condoms?" I asked.

"Yes, babe." He kissed me before rolling it down his length. "You still don't want to get pregnant as a teenager, right?"

"Right. I just... figured guys hated those."

"Not as much as unexpected surprises that last for eighteen years."

Truthfully, I was taken aback that he would consider it without me having to say anything. In my experience, guys didn't care about birth control. They could just disappear and leave the woman to deal with it on her own.

But Connor wasn't like that. I had to remember that he wasn't anything like the men I knew growing up.

I leaned forward to kiss him, giving him my appreciation without words. He caressed my back and my ass, positioning his head at my slick entrance.

"You're in control, babe," he murmured into my neck. "Take what you need from me."

I needed all of him, completely. But as I started lowering myself onto him, his girth and my lack of any recent sexual activity became clear.

Connor responded immediately to my discomfort. He pressed a thumb to my clit and kissed his way down my chest to take a nipple in his mouth. His tongue and finger swirled hypnotically on those two sensitive points. When his teeth grazed the aching peak, I gasped, squirmed, and unwittingly impaled myself further down his cock.

He moved on to my other nipple as I stretched around

him, my pussy already convulsing from him working my clit. It was too good, almost too much. I braced my hands on his chest as he slowly filled me, driving me to the edge with every inch of him.

When he was finally seated within me, every cell and hair follicle felt abuzz with sensitivity. He was inside me and not just physically. I felt him in every pore.

"Oh God, Mel," he groaned as I made the slightest shifting movements. "You feel so fucking good."

He filled me up so completely I didn't want to move much. He also felt so right inside me, I didn't want to be deprived of him.

Gradually, I thrust back on him harder. He began driving his hips up into me as I adjusted to him, holding my waist as we crashed together in the middle.

It felt like slow, beautiful violence. He sliced through me, but I couldn't get enough. When the pleasure teetered over the line to pain, he cupped my face and kissed me so sweetly to bring me back. When I started whimpering and my whole body quivered for release, he bucked into me relentlessly to hit my clit in just the right way.

When I came, I released so much through that orgasm. I released everything I felt about him, from the love growing in my heart to the annoyance and frustration from him being a pain in my ass. It was blissful, cathartic, and felt like a weight lifted off my chest.

"Did I hurt you, babe?" Connor brushed kisses across my cheeks. I didn't even realize I shed tears until I tasted their saltiness on his lips.

"No, you didn't." I smiled through my panting, ragged breaths. "That was just... really good."

"You're welcome," he chuckled into my neck as he

lazily rolled us over, pressing my back into the mattress with the depth of his kisses.

After a few moments to catch my breath, he sheathed himself inside me with a hot moan and took my breath away all over again.

His weight on top of me felt incredible, so secure and intimate. I wrapped my arms around his wide back as he thrust into me with those powerful thighs. He lifted my hips higher as he crashed into my clit, building another orgasm through me as I barely recovered from the first one.

"God, Mel, you feel incredible," he growled, picking up speed and power as he grew impossibly stiff within me.

"Connor, you...ohh..." I lost all ability to make words as another orgasm shattered me.

His release came with one final, deep thrust into me with a powerful roar. We held each other so tightly, our skin carried matching red marks when we finally pulled away.

❧ 8 ❧

MELODY

"I swear to God you're *trying* to poke my eye out with that thing!"

"Then quit walking behind me. Get up here next to me, babe."

I ran up next to Connor and laced my fingers through his outstretched hand. He brought the back of my palm to his lips and nothing could calm the resulting fluttering in my heart.

The angry-slash-makeup sex took so much out of us, we ended up napping most of the day away. We woke up just as evening settled in, and Connor suggested I join him for practice after dinner.

Just like the first time, I followed him into the woods and far away from any curious eyes. Only this time we were under cool, silver moonlight instead of blazing hot sun. I was starting to think I could get used to being a night owl. Daytime was so overrated. Nighttime had such an unappreciated beauty and romance to it.

I had a flashlight, so we weren't just lit by moonlight,

thankfully. Connor seemed oddly excited about practicing in the dark, though.

"Ever tried balancing on one leg with your eyes closed?" he asked.

"Sounds hard," I muttered.

"Exactly. You can always find new ways to challenge yourself," he said. "And the more you challenge yourself, the more you improve."

"Whatever, weirdo," I teased, giving him a sloppy kiss on the cheek.

He spent the next few minutes telling me all about the different kinds of push-ups and exercises they made him do in the Marines, when I saw an unmistakable flash of white in the corner of my eye.

At this point, I was essentially expecting it and stopped walking abruptly, turning to face the direction of the movement.

"Babe?" Connor's grip tightened on my hand. "Did you see something?"

"Yeah," I answered, remembering what Razvan said and tried to project my voice loudly. "I know you're out there. I'm not sure why you're hiding, but please show yourself. I'm not afraid and you know we won't hurt you."

I sounded way more confident than I felt. Nothing answered me for a few moments, and Connor leaned down to whisper in my ear.

"Babe, who're you—FUCK!" He grabbed my arm and pulled me back protectively when the beautiful, pale man came into view.

With his long, platinum hair and graceful stride he looked ethereal and haunting, like moonlight itself. His long, lean-muscled torso was bare except for the angry red burns on his chest and ribs. He looked incredibly tall as he approached us from the brush, at least six foot four. For a moment I wondered if he was naked, but to my relief he wore dark jeans, although his feet were bare.

The beautiful pale man from my dream stood before me in the flesh, but this time I wasn't afraid. I still didn't know why he morphed like a reptile or why he spoke to me like I was someone else, but after getting past the initial fear, instinctually, I knew he wasn't here to harm us.

Those sad, golden eyes looked at me with recognition, and I knew instantly who he was.

"Who the hell are you?"

Connor apparently did not.

"It's okay, Con." I pulled my arm gently out of his grip and stepped toward the ghostly man. "What's your name?"

"My name is Hunter." I did not expect such a deep, masculine voice to come out of such a man. "My children are Roo and Rinna."

I smiled. That confirmed it. I felt crazy, but the proof was standing right in front of me. A giddy excitedness bloomed in my chest.

"Connor," I whispered. "This is who we helped to escape from Drowningville."

He looked at me and then back at Hunter, looking more confused with each passing second.

"How... what?"

"Hunter," I said, feeling like some sort of mediator. "Thank you for coming out and talking to us. Would you like to come sit down so we can clear the air?"

He lowered his golden eyes, and I saw his lips twitch in what appeared to be a smile of relief.

"Yes. Thank you, Melody."

"Call me Mel," I said automatically.

The three of us sat around a cluster of boulders not far from where Hunter decided to reveal himself. Connor stayed glued to my side while eyeing Hunter suspiciously, not that I could blame him. Hunter kept a respectful distance away. I could tell he was trying to appear as non-threatening as possible—seemingly a challenge with his imposing frame and predatory stalking skills.

"So *you're* the fucking wolf man?" Connor demanded.

"Yes." Hunter's lip curled with distaste at the nickname. "I don't care for being called that, but I was the one on display, drugged, beaten, and electrocuted. I recognized you both from the crowd, and then in the trailer when I woke up later."

"What would you prefer us to call you?" I asked gently, resting a hand on Connor's arm to calm him.

"Humans have called us all sorts of things," he mused. "Lycan is what our kind call each other. Wolf shifter is also appropriate and a simple explanation."

"You're saying you're *not* human?" Connor said incredulously.

Hunter's eyes flashed with amusement. "Right now, I'm just as human as you are, Connor." He tilted his head as though a canine would. "And yet I'm completely different from you."

"You can... turn into a wolf, can't you?" It sounded absolutely insane coming out of my mouth.

He fixated those golden eyes on me. "Yes. My form is fully human like this," he gestured to himself, "or fully wolf. That form you saw me in was... forced. It's an in-between state and not natural for us to look like that."

"Can you tell us how you ended up there?" I asked. My

heart ached with the memory of seeing him, human in stature but covered in white fur, elongated ears, and an extended snout. His kids looked the same. Goddamn, they forced *kids* to look like that for entertainment.

While the old anger and horror flooded my veins, Connor visibly relaxed next to me and rubbed my back.

"We were captured maybe three weeks ago," Hunter began. "These carnivals hire poachers specifically to hunt shifters for a massive bounty. They must have stalked my pack for months and covered their scent well. One day, they finally ambushed us and we got separated from everyone else."

He let out a heavy sigh before continuing. "It was just Roo, Rinna, and me. We were outnumbered, so I shifted to human to try and bargain with them." He swallowed. "There was a language barrier, but I asked them to spare my children if I went along willingly. They seemed to understand and agree. But they still tranquilized me anyway. The next thing I knew, I woke up tied up in a cage, stuck between my wolf and human form. My kids were right there with me."

"I'm so sorry," I choked. My throat felt like it was closing up, and Connor kissed my temple as he rubbed soothing circles on my back.

"It's okay. We're all safe now, thanks to you." Hunter offered a small smile. "I was in and out of consciousness for what had to be days. They injected all of us with something that kept us stuck between shifts. My poor kids didn't understand. I hate that I couldn't protect them."

"There was nothing you could do," Connor said sympathetically. "We saw how they treated you. It was absolutely barbaric."

"You left, I assume to be reunited with your pack," I said. "Why are you still here?"

Hunter's face fell. "Yes, I've been looking for them these past few days, but haven't picked up a fresh scent. My worst fear is they all got captured." He looked up. "With nowhere for us to go, I figured the least I could do was watch over those who saved us. I stayed hidden because I didn't know if you would understand."

"I don't know how, but... I do," I said softly. "For some reason, I *had* to see you and then rescue you. Not doing it wasn't an option."

"Clearly not," Connor teased me affectionately.

"Whatever the reason, I'll always be grateful to you both." Hunter rested his gaze solemnly on us. "If not for my own life, for my children's. This has been traumatic for them, but they'll grow up wild and free like they were meant to."

"Where are they now?" I asked.

"I made a small den for us in the woods." Hunter's eyes lit up. "If you'd like, I can bring them by and formally introduce you later."

"I'd like that," I smiled before another, less comfortable thought occurred to me. "Do they, um, have a mother?"

"My mate was killed by hunters a few years ago, not long after Rinna was born," He frowned. "Roo remembers her but Rinna doesn't, really."

An ache gripped my chest. That was who he had to be talking to in my dream. I still couldn't shake the feeling that it was wrong to be there. How would I even begin to explain the dreams to him?

"Fuck, I'm sorry. They're so young and have had it so rough already."

"They've been okay. We've always had the pack around to raise them. As for now?" He sighed, but warmth and pride tugged at a smile on his lips. "They're so strong. They've inspired me to keep going."

"That's great to hear." Warmth and relief spread through me. This family was okay. It would take time and some healing, but they would be okay in the end. That was all I wanted to happen when we broke them out.

"Are there others like you?" Connor asked. "Obviously you have your pack, but are there other... animal shifters? You talked about these poachers like they're a common thing."

"Yes. Nearly every animal you can imagine, there are shifters of," Hunter answered. "Well, vertebrates, at least. The theory is shifters developed early during evolution when the first vertebrates began splitting off into different species. Some carried only the human genes, some became only the non-human animals. Others carried both, developing abilities of two distinct animals at the same time."

He looked pointedly at me. "The one who you were talking to earlier today. He's a shifter as well."

"Razvan?" My eyes widened. Was *that* why I was so drawn to him? My curiosity toward him and Hunter felt nearly the same. Now that I knew what they both looked like in human form, that curiosity gave way to a magnetic, inexplicable attraction.

Hunter was almost painfully handsome, with otherworldly features like a model. Razvan had a unique look too, which his many tattoos just enhanced, but he was dark where Hunter was light. Still, I felt a nearly equal pull to both of them.

"I knew there was something weird about that guy," Conner said. "No offense," he added to Hunter.

"Trust me," Hunter smiled. "Weird is one of the least offensive things you could call me."

"Do you know what animal he shifts to?" I asked.

"I can make an educated guess based on his smell," Hunter said with a stroke of his short beard. "But it's not my place to tell. There are so many shifters among humans staying hidden for their own protection."

I nodded in understanding. It would seem I'd be talking to Razvan again soon. His vague hints made a lot more sense now, along with his reason for being so evasive.

"He is free, which is surprising to see why he's still a performer," Hunter said with clear distaste. "Most of us in the carnival are not here willingly."

"That's horrible," I lamented. "How can this be allowed to happen? Why isn't anyone causing an uproar about that? It's basically slavery."

"Because so few believe we exist," he answered sadly. "There are no laws to protect us when we're invisible. The carnivals and circuses pay a lot of money to ensure that we don't become common knowledge. It keeps our value high when people still aren't sure we're real."

"And that's the reason for the drugs, I bet," Connor said. "To make you look like, well, a circus freak. Otherwise you're just an ordinary person or an animal, which is not as interesting."

"Exactly," Hunter nodded.

The three of us sat in silence for a moment, Connor and I absorbing this mind-blowing information while

Hunter watched us curiously. Even in human form, he was a lot like a wolf in a way. His golden eyes were intense, wise, and wild. They seemed to notice things our human eyes couldn't perceive.

"Well, this has been... something," Connor breathed with a shake of his head. "I knew this business was fucked, but straight up hunting people and treating them worse than animals? It's just sick."

I looked at him. "Has Nigel ever...?"

"Not that I know of," he said. "Nigel's a decent guy. I'd be surprised if he even knows about it. In my two years in this business I've never known about this, not even rumors."

"The one you spoke of earlier, Razvan," Hunter chimed in. "I don't know him, but I can't imagine a shifter working willingly with a manager that has enslaved others like us. And I haven't smelled any others around. Those are all good signs that this one hasn't sunk that low. Yet."

He rose fluidly from his boulder, standing to his full, towering height. His muscles on his long frame were slender and lithe. Where Connor could be a bodybuilder, Hunter could've been a swimmer. I wondered how he looked in wolf form.

"I'm glad I got to meet you both, formally," he said. "I have to catch dinner for the kids so I'll leave you two for now."

"Please bring them by the camp," I said. "I'd love to meet them and see how they're doing."

"I will," Hunter promised. His smile and golden gaze lingered on me long enough to make my stomach flutter before his shift began.

White fur sprouted across his body as bones popped

and rearranged themselves. He dropped to all fours as he passed the point of where we first saw him. In mere moments, all human features disappeared and a huge, beautiful white wolf stood before us.

"Holy shit," Connor breathed.

Hunter wagged his tail and approached us, closer than he'd ever been. I held my hand out, and he sniffed it with his cool, black nose and gave me a small lick.

"Wow, you're so beautiful," I said, forgetting momentarily I was not just complimenting a gorgeous animal but a *person*.

Hunter let out a high-pitched yip that sounded like a laugh. I felt myself turning beet red with embarrassment. He gave me another affectionate lick before running off into the woods. Connor and I watched his sleek, white form elegantly slink away into the darkness.

"Well, damn." Connor rubbed his face. "I don't think I can focus on practice after all that."

9

MELODY

onnor and I spotted Razvan the next evening in the tavern at dinnertime. He was alone for once, without his crew or a fawning woman in sight. Eating his plate of food quietly and drinking from his pint glass, he seemed different without an entourage. Almost pensive and introverted with no one to show off for.

"Should we go talk to him?" I asked Connor. "About, you know, shifter stuff?"

"That's all you, babe." He nudged me in Razvan's direction gently. "Go ahead, I'll hang out with Nigel."

I turned to give him a look, but he was already heading off in the opposite direction, leaving me standing there with my bowl of stew and glass of Coke.

With a sigh and a big dose of courage, I walked up to the table where the tattooed, steel-eyed man sat by himself.

"This seat taken?" I asked.

His demeanor changed immediately, his face lighting up with an electric smile. "It is now by you, *steluţa*."

My pulse thrumming nervously in my veins, I stepped over the picnic bench and sat down in front of him. To distract myself, I took a long swig of Coke, suddenly feeling very thirsty.

"To what do I owe the pleasure of this dinner date?" He took a bite of his charred steak and chewed slowly, his eyes dancing with amusement.

"I met, um," I lowered my voice to a whisper and leaned across the table, "my admirer you told me about the other day."

His eyebrows lifted in surprise, and his smile faded slightly. "I see. So you know what he is?"

I nodded. "I take it you do too?"

"He smelled canine," was the answer. "So some kind of wolf or dog. Probably wolf, since no mere domesticated pooch is worthy of you."

"Yes, he's a wolf," I confirmed, brushing off the flattery.

"And you've never seen anything like him before?"

I shook my head. "Never in my life."

A corner of his mouth lifted into a smirk. "But you were not frightened?"

I shook my head again and drained my cup of Coke until it was empty. Holy shit, I couldn't believe this conversation was actually happening. My throat would not stop drying out.

"Ah, that won't do," Razvan said, referring to my empty cup. "What're you drinking, *steluța*? I'll get you another."

"Coke, thanks," I answered.

He shook his head slowly while clicking his tongue at me. "I'll get you some Jack to go with it."

"Please don't," I said. "I don't drink."

"Oh, that's right. I remember." He gave me a curious look. "Why not?"

I glared at him. "Not something I'm up for discussing."

"Now who's being evasive, *steluţa?*" he teased.

"Okay, what the hell is that name you keep calling me?" I demanded. "You won't stop using it so you must find it especially fitting for me."

"That I do," he grinned. "I'll tell you what it means if you tell me why you don't drink."

There it was. That cocky attitude was back. Infuriating and also stupidly sexy, which only made me even more frustrated.

"Those two things aren't even close to being equal," I spat.

"I know that. Even so, it's just a simple exchange of information."

"Some name you're calling me does not hold the same amount of weight as my reason for not drinking."

"How do you know that?" he asked with the same infuriating calmness. "You don't know the meaning of the word."

For a moment, I forgot all about why I came over to talk to him in the first place. He wound me up like a spring just for the fun of it. And if we didn't get off this topic soon, I was going to explode. Probably by throwing food in his face.

"Let's go back to that other thing we were talking about," I said through gritted teeth, stabbing at the chopped carrots and potatoes in my stew.

"Oh no, you're not escaping me that easily."

Out of nowhere, a heavy weight pressed down on my beat-up sneaker. It didn't hurt but startled the shit out of me, to where I flung my spoon down to the floor. I couldn't believe it just from feeling it, so I had to glance under the table to see.

"Are you playing footsy with me?"

His laugh was playful, musical, carefree, and I hated it.

"I won't judge you for the reasons you don't drink, *steluţa*," he said. "It might surprise you to learn that I'm a very sympathetic listener."

There was no way I was getting out of this. Damn it. Not even Connor knew, not really.

"My mother is an alcoholic," I said, lowering my voice again. Right away, Razvan's face grew serious. "She did everything she could to be as drunk as possible as often as possible. We often went without food or utilities because she spent every disability check on booze."

"I'm sorry, Melody. I didn't realize." His voice was sympathetic. It was soothing to hear and telling him was more cathartic than I expected.

"It wasn't just that." Once I started talking, it seemed impossible to stop. "She brought all kinds of men home. Alcoholics just like her. And sometimes like her, they'd just pass out after a while and be completely useless. Other times, they got violent."

Razvan growled and clenched his fists on the table. I got a distinct whiff of a burning smell and looked up. My eyes widened when I realized small wisps of smoke were coming from his mouth and nostrils. Maybe I shouldn't have been surprised, knowing he was some kind of shifter, but at the moment I was completely stunned and clueless.

He opened his hands and coughed, waving away the smoke casually.

"Sorry," he said a bit sheepishly. "I get a bit protective of innocent people who get hurt."

"It's okay. I guess I should get used to, um, not entirely *human* reactions."

He smiled again, but this time it was warm and genuine instead of teasing. "Go on, Melody."

"Well, yeah. That's kind of the gist of it. I saw what drinking did to my mom and the kids at school were sure to let me know how trashy and fucked up my family was."

"You're *not* trashy," he snarled.

"Well, that *is* how I grew up," I explained. "We lived in a trailer, not even a real house. My mom also kept getting pregnant and having more kids than she could afford. But she figured out more kids meant more money from the government, which meant more booze."

"Fucking hell," he cursed.

"In a science class," I went on. "I learned that addictions are often genetic and can be passed from parent to child. My older sister followed right in my mom's footsteps, so that was enough proof for me. I swore I'd never touch alcohol after that."

"And you've held strong I see, despite all these pesky men offering it to you," he winked. "That's admirable for someone your age."

"Something tells me you're old enough to know better." I stuck my tongue out at him.

"I'm twenty-three, so I can get away with youthful ignorance for a bit longer," he joked back, relaxing with one tattooed arm propped against the wall behind him. "But thank you for telling me, Melody," he added with a gentleness I had yet to hear from him. "That is a deeply personal and valid reason. I won't push it on you anymore."

His grin returned. "Except when you deserve a little ribbing, maybe."

"I don't think I've ever really talked about my past to someone else," I admitted. "It felt good to get off my chest."

He raised an eyebrow quizzically. "Not even your man?"

I hesitated. "No, I was planning to, but I haven't yet. And he's not my man."

Both eyebrows lifted in surprise. "No?"

"It's complicated," I admitted. "We're together but he doesn't want me to limit myself to him."

He leaned back, lifting his chin as he looked at me. It seemed I was full of surprises tonight.

"And is that what *you* want?"

"I don't know," I sighed.

How did we turn to this topic? Connor grounded me and helped everything to make sense, yet confused the fuck out of me at the same time. We were clearly attracted to each other. The pleasant soreness in my body from yesterday and this morning proved that. I was falling for him, and he clearly was developing some feelings for me, too.

But then he pushed me away, saying he didn't want to label us as anything. And that stung, as much as I swallowed my pride and tried being cool with it. I couldn't figure out if he genuinely didn't feel worthy of me, which was bullshit, or he was trying to keep his own options open.

I still hadn't mentioned anything about that message I saw on his phone back in Drowningville. Someone named Vicky texted him asking, "Are you ever going to talk to me again?" He mentioned an ex-fiancee that left him, and I couldn't get rid of the nagging feeling that he'd go back to her if he could.

"Well, if you don't like limits," Razvan spread his hands out suggestively, "that's something else we have in common."

I rolled my eyes. "Not happening. So are you going to tell me what that word means now?"

"*Steluța,*" he said again, enunciating it slowly. Watching his mouth move to speak the foreign word was incredibly erotic. "It means little star."

I blinked, taken aback. That was not what I was expecting. It sounded... cute.

"And why have you chosen to call me that, of all things?"

"Because," he said softly. "You are small but shine so brightly. It came to me the moment I saw you."

"I'd say you were sweet if I didn't know you were also a pervert."

His head dipped back as he laughed uproariously, the dark tattoos on his neck jumping as if joining in and laughing with him. "Why can't I be both?"

My face heated under his smoldering gaze. Damn it. He was flirting again, and I didn't know what to do.

"I suppose you can be," I mumbled awkwardly.

He recovered from laughing, and a calm seriousness swept over him.

"When you're done eating, I supposed you'd like to talk a bit more about shifter things."

I nodded. "If you'd like to."

He leaned forward, his eyes keeping their hold on me like some kind of alien tractor beam.

"I don't trust many humans, but I feel I can trust you, *steluța*," he whispered. "You're not shifter but you're not quite like other humans. You smell different somehow."

"I'm not sure if I should take that as a compliment," I frowned.

His lips spread into a smirk as he chuckled. "Oh, it's not a bad smell. Not in the slightest."

"That's good to know." I picked at my stew, no longer feeling an appetite. The burning curiosity to learn about him consumed me. "To be honest, Razvan, I feel like I'm starting to trust you too."

His eyes widened so much, I wondered for a moment if I offended him. Then his smirk bloomed into a full-on grin. "That means more to me than you could possibly know, *steluța*."

10

MELODY

azvan and I got up to leave the tavern after a few more minutes of small talk and picking at our food. I looked around for Connor to tell him, but the place was getting so crowded that I lost sight of him.

He'll know who I'm with. He practically forced me to talk to him, I figured.

Raz was quiet as we walked side-by-side to the Renaissance fair vendors near where I first saw him juggling those knives.

"That thing you did with fire," I said, breaking our silence. "That's part of your shifter abilities?"

"Yes," he answered quietly, but didn't elaborate.

I let the information turn over in my head as we put more distance between us and the lights of the carnival.

"I don't want to frighten you, *steluța*," he said as our steps slowed to a halt. "My shift is not an ordinary animal. So I'm going to do this in small steps."

For the first time since I met him, he seemed insecure.

Unsure of himself. He looked genuinely like he might have regretted bringing me out here.

"Okay," I said, trying to give a reassuring smile.

His mouth only tensed. "Please don't scream. It'll attract attention."

"I promise I won't," I answered. "Hunter—the wolf I met, told me how shifters have a high value and are exploited by carnivals. He said it was surprising that you're still performing freely and willingly."

"That is an entirely different story," Raz said dryly. "But yes, if people see me and know who and what I am, I'll be no better than a caged animal again. I'm essentially putting my freedom in your hands, Melody."

"I understand," I told him solemnly. "I won't alert you to anyone. I promise."

He still looked hesitant for a moment before nodding sharply.

"You might want to stand a few feet away," he warned.

I backed away from him a few steps, my heart thrumming with anticipation.

Razvan nervously exhaled a deep breath. "This is how I was forced to perform when I was first captured."

In the darkness, I didn't see any changes. I didn't even hear the sound of bones crunching and popping like when Hunter shifted. But when he stepped into the dim light casting through the trees, I barely recognized him.

His skin turned entirely black and was covered in a fine layer of what looked like scales. New bumps and ridges emerged on his skin like horns or spikes trying to poke through. His teeth grew a couple inches longer, poking past his lips, and all sharply pointed. And his eyes! Still steely gray but now with a slitted, reptilian pupil.

"Holy shit, Razvan," I breathed, taking a step forward.

"Don't come closer," he warned, holding up a scaly hand with long black claws. His words still came out clearly, but with a different pitch to his voice.

"You don't look that different," I said carefully, drinking in his new appearance with fascination. "Just... more modified."

He nodded. "I was first advertised as a lizard-man. Just a regular guy with full-body scales tattooed, filed teeth, and some subdermal implants. They injected me with drugs to keep my shift at this exact spot."

"You're still mostly human," I observed.

"Correct," he confirmed. "But eventually that wasn't enough. An ordinary human wasn't bringing in enough money. So they made me shift to this point and advertised me as a *real* lizard-man."

He calmly removed his vest and stood shirtless before me, displaying more of the bumps and ridges on his ribs and chest. Then I heard the bones crunching, the organs shifting, and what sounded like skin tearing apart.

I gasped, bringing my hand to my mouth only because it sounded so painful. But while the creature in front of me was unlike anything I'd ever seen, it still didn't scare me.

Razvan still retained some human features, but was mostly reptilian at this stage. Large, bat-like wings sprouted from his back. Actual horns and spikes sprouted all over his body. His black scales looked like shimmery obsidian.

Our eyes met, and I could see the apprehension in his barely human face. He opened his jaws—now elongated and slender, allowing soft wisps of smoke to gently curl out and create a type of aura around his head.

"No way," I whispered in awe, the realization hitting me like a brick. "You're... a *dragon?*"

He nodded, which looked a bit weird because of how his neck muscles rearranged, but I was too busy being utterly fascinated to care.

"That is so freaking cool!" I giggled like a high-schooler, unable to contain how thrilled I was to be seeing this happen. A goddamn dragon! An animal that wasn't supposed to exist except in mythology and folklore!

The initial shock of shifters existing at all seemed to wear off after seeing Hunter. Now I was fixated on every one of Razvan's scales, his pointy teeth, and those glorious, beautiful wings.

He finished the shift, falling to all fours as all his human features sank and disappeared into his dragon body. He grew to the size of a large pickup truck. A long, whip-like tail completed the ensemble, and I was standing in front of a real fucking dragon.

"Amazing," I breathed, unable to take my eyes off him, let alone believe what I was seeing. "Can you still under-stand me?"

Razvan huffed a breath through his nostrils and bobbed his head down in an affirmative.

Hesitantly, I outstretched my hand. "Is it okay if I touch you?"

He paused for a moment, as if unsure, then slowly extended his nose out to my palm.

My fingers touched armor-tough scales that were warm, almost hot on contact. It felt like holding a warm cup of coffee, if such a cup was scaly.

I couldn't stop grinning and giggling as I looked into those gray, slitted-pupil eyes. I scratched under his jaw and Razvan made a low rumbling sound, almost like a purr. Those eyes closed halfway, as if in pleasure.

"I can't believe you're real," I whispered, taking in every claw, horn, and ridge that adorned him. "This is absolutely amazing."

He grunted and settled his belly down on the ground, folding his wings against his back and curling his rear legs underneath.

"I'd love to see you fly," I told him, gazing at his wings. "That would be incredible to see. I bet you can't do it often, though. Too risky."

His head jerked down again in a sharp nod. I brought my hand back to my side and, to my surprise, he bumped it with his nose. It seemed affectionate, like a nuzzle.

"Yeah, you like that?" I laughed, scratching under his jaw again. I had to mentally remind myself again this was a person, not just an animal. Would I be okay with doing this to him in human form? I couldn't be sure. All I knew was, as a dragon, he really liked chin scratches.

With a final huff and rumble, he pulled away after a few moments and I heard the distinct, somewhat grotesque sounds of shifting again. In the next moment, Razvan the handsome, heavily tattooed human, picked up his vest from the ground without a word and slid his arms through it.

When he looked at me, it was a look of apprehension and uncertainty.

"What's wrong?" I asked. "That was incredible!"

"You really think so?" he asked in disbelief.

"Yes!" I cried, then quickly lowered my voice. "I have

so many questions! Are all dragons shifters? Why are they considered a fantasy creature nowadays? How awesome is it to fly and breathe fire?"

Razvan chuckled, shoving his hands in his jean pockets and lowering his eyes to the ground. If I didn't know any better, I'd say he was being shy.

"Yes, dragons only exist as shifters," he said quietly. "We are few and far between. It's strange and gratifying to hear you say such kind words. Among my people, we are considered cursed and undesirable."

"How is that possible?" I demanded. "You're a human and yet so much more."

"Thousands of years of folklore and superstition," he shrugged. "What made it even worse for me was that I'm a firstborn son. I had responsibilities to carry on the family name. When my shifting abilities came to light as a toddler, my family saw it as a punishment from God."

"That's awful," I breathed, stepping closer to him. "I'm so sorry."

"They forced me to hide it, and I tried as best I could," he went on. "But being a shifter is like having two personalities. My dragon is a part of me, yet separate. He has strong instincts and desires apart from my own. I can always feel him, even now." He tapped his chest gently. "And he can't stay hidden for long or he'll go mad. As a teenager, the more I tried to hold him back, the more he fought me for control. I would go to bed as a human and wake up flying over the clouds."

"So you *have* to shift, at least every once in a while," I concluded.

"Exactly," he confirmed. "My dragon started lashing out. Unable to control him, I'd grow horns or wings and a tail while out in broad daylight. Eventually, my parents had enough. They felt they had to get rid of me to lift the curse off our family."

I hardly dared to ask. "What did they do?"

"They sold me to a carnival."

Fuck. Just like Hunter. A person treated like livestock. The thought made me physically ill and my heart couldn't seem to take all the pain of feeling for these people. It almost made me wish I didn't feel so much at all.

Even so, my empathy was nothing compared to what they went through. Hunter and Razvan's story at least seemed to have happier endings.

"But you're free now," I pointed out. "But still in the carnival. How did that happen?"

He smiled at me in a way that made my heart flutter. "A story for another time, *steluţa*. We should get you back before people wonder where the ringmistress ran off to."

It only then registered to me how late it had gotten. Dusk had settled into darkness with the sky brilliantly alight with stars.

"You can walk me straight home if you'd like," I offered. "We have an early morning meeting with Nigel and I want to be refreshed before showing my mad ringmistress skills." I punctuated that last statement with an eye-roll which got a laugh out of Razvan.

"You'll be great," he said warmly. "And I'll be happy to escort you home."

We took the narrow path back to camp side-by-side, closer than our first walk through the woods but still without touching. I found myself enjoying his flirty small talk and teasing, laughing as we came into the clearing a few minutes later, but still feeling unsure about touching him.

I wanted to smack him lightly for teasing me, or to simply run my fingers along the lines of ink on his skin but held myself back. Why did I have no problem touching him as a dragon but felt incredibly bashful doing so while human? Even though they were the same, my brain still separated touching another person and touching an animal.

We walked to my camp to find Connor waiting by the fire. He sat in his lawn chair, staring at the dancing flames. An empty six-pack of beer sat on the ground next to his chair. He rested one nearly-empty bottle on his knee as his eyes darted up to meet us.

"Hey babe," he said in a flat tone. "I was wondering when you'd come back."

A cold chill swept over me, and my whole body bristled with tension. If he wasn't drinking, I'd be ready to handle whatever jealous, snappish remarks he'd throw out. But just seeing those bottles made me brace myself for impact, whether that was from words or fists.

Logically, I knew Connor wouldn't hurt me. But my nervous system kicked into protection mode, anyway. My body responded to the sight and smell of alcohol like an allergic reaction. Shut down. Be quiet. Protect. Do not provoke.

It was Razvan's gentle fingertips on my lower back that reminded me he was still there.

"Go on to bed, *steluța*," he said. "I think it's time Connor and I got to know each other."

I looked at him in surprise and was met with his carefree, easygoing smile.

"We'll behave. I promise," he said with a gentle push toward the trailer door. "Sweet dreams, *steluţa*."

"Um, goodnight." I glanced at Connor, who didn't meet my eyes. Great. Drunk and in one of his moods. I looked back at Razvan. "Thanks for walking with me."

"Thank you for not running away and screaming," he returned with a chuckle.

I went inside and got undressed for bed without bothering to turn the lights on. My weariness overpowered the burning curiosity to know what those two would be talking about.

I fell asleep to the deep, rumbling murmur of men's voices outside.

CONNOR

I watched warily as the tattooed man took a seat across the fire from me. He eyed my six-pack but didn't ask for one. I was a few beers deep at that point and felt surly enough to not bother offering.

"Something you want to discuss?" I asked, keeping my tone light but firm. I was willing to hear him out, but would not stand for any bullshit concerning Mel.

In the back of my mind, I knew he wasn't that bad of a guy. Hell, I practically pushed Mel to spend time with him. But after she walked off with him and the minutes ticked by with no sign of either of them, the nagging doubts started creeping in. I was only lightly buzzed, but the beers definitely made it worse.

When I saw them finally walking back, I was equally relieved and jealous that she was smiling and giggling. She was happy and unhurt, but I knew men. I knew so many of them played a nice act until they got a woman's defenses down. They wouldn't hurt her until she felt too attached to leave.

Razvan's steely gray eyes flickered from my booze to my face. "You might want to watch your consumption around her."

Oh, damn. This guy had balls.

"Fuckin' excuse me?" I demanded, keeping my voice low. "After a nice stroll through the woods, suddenly *you* know what's best for her?"

"It's not hard to see if you use your eyes," he answered calmly. "She was fine and relaxed right up until she saw you. You must know she doesn't drink."

"Yeah, and?" I challenged. "I don't force it on her. If she doesn't like me having a couple, she can say so. She's a big girl."

"She is, and yet she's like a child in other ways. I can smell her fear and anxiety around alcohol. It's an automatic reaction."

"How the hell do you know?" I challenged. "Did she tell you something?"

"A small bit, yes," he admitted.

"What did she say?" My jealousy flared up like a green-eyed monster inside me. She shared something with *him* that she didn't with me?

"That's for her to tell. Not me." Razvan's arms rested on the knees of his scuffed, dark jeans and his voice never wavered. He was utterly relaxed and not intimidated by me at all. I had to give him an ounce of respect for that.

I sank back in my chair. It was my own fault Mel hadn't completely opened up to me, as much as I didn't want to admit it. I protected her and would never harm her, but I still scared her. She watched her words around me and tried not to set me off. That wasn't fair to her.

The first time we made love, I was pissed and jealous

for no good reason. She stood her ground, but I saw even her resolve weakening in those big doe eyes. And despite our beautiful, intimate moment, I saw her guard go back up. Especially when I brushed off the boyfriend title again.

I wanted to be officially hers so fucking badly. But why did *I* deserve that when she let her guard down to the tattooed punk sitting across from me?

"So you're a shifter too, huh?" I mumbled, changing the subject.

He looked up, his eyes wide with surprise. "You know?"

"Yes. Seems she didn't tell you everything after all." I quickly relayed our rescue of the wolves back in Drowningville, then getting reacquainted with them again here in Crying Falls.

"Craziest shit I ever seen," I said, draining the rest of my last beer. That would be the last one I had for a while. For Mel, I'd take his advice to heart. "Honestly, I'm not surprised by how this industry has treated y'all. It's sickening, but any chance to make a buck, they'll take."

He blinked a few times, scratching a hand over his scalp as if he still couldn't believe I knew about him.

"So you a wolf too, or something else?" I asked.

He laughed. "No, I'm not a wolf. Think more... reptilian." His eyes met mine and his smile faded into seriousness. "Forgive me for being evasive. I'm just not used to humans knowing. And my shift is, well, shocking to most people. To say the least."

"Fair enough," I answered, settling back into my chair.

"I showed Mel what I am," he said, barely above a whisper. "That's why we went away from everyone. Nothing else happened. I just shifted, and we came straight back."

"Okay." I believed him. The more we talked, the more the jealousy subsided.

"She... was not shocked. Or frightened." He seemed dumbfounded as he said that. "She was *excited*. She was smiling and laughing. I've never had that reaction from someone before. It's usually screams and running. Sometimes fainting."

I gave him a confused look. "Dude, are you a fucking dinosaur or some shit?"

He laughed again. "You're not too far off." With a smirk, he added, "I have a feeling you'll find out sooner rather than later."

"That's entirely up to you, man," I said. "But yeah, Mel is different. She seems... I dunno, *in tune* with you shifter folks. With the wolves, she knew right away they were like people. Intelligent, understanding of language and behavior, protective of their kids. Me and every other person in there obviously had no fucking clue."

"You're different too, Connor," he piped up.

"Me? How?" I asked, taken aback.

"Just the fact that you know what I am and we're still sitting here having a conversation like two normal people? You have no idea how big of a deal that is." He leaned forward emphatically. "Every human who's found out about me has either been scared shitless or tried to kill me. You smell like an ordinary human, but the fact that you've had neither of those reactions to me says there's something different in your biology."

"I have been scared shitless," I admitted. "And I... have killed."

When Razvan narrowed his eyes in confusion, I pulled my dog tags out of my shirt. Before I could rethink it, I also lifted my pant leg to show the metal rod of my prosthetic leg.

I knew a big secret about him now. I figured if we both cared for Mel, it only made sense for me to be honest with him too.

"Ah." His eyebrows lifted as he leaned back and rubbed his jaw. "That makes a lot of sense now."

"Yeah, just a walking redneck stereotype," I cracked.

"If that's what you are, I'm just a punk ass Romanian," he grinned.

"So what are your intentions with Mel?" I asked, turning serious again.

"What are you, her father now?" he scoffed in response.

"No," I shook my head. "I won't keep her on a leash. I won't snoop or get in y'alls business. But I've seen how you act with the other women here. You can't blame a guy for being protective."

"What are *your* intentions with her?" he retorted. "She's with you but said things were complicated."

"To say the least," I muttered in agreement.

He spread his hands out and looked from side to side. "What am I supposed to do with that information?"

"Does it really matter to you if a woman is taken or not?" I challenged. "You came right up to her in front of me before you knew anything about us. She shot you down hard."

"I don't like that word, *taken*. I've never felt that women belonged to men, nor the other way around." He bit back another grin. "A woman who wants me will choose me whether she has another man or not. And I can choose her in return or spend my time elsewhere."

"Mel can't be used and discarded like that," I growled. "She needs stability, people she can rely on. She has too much of a heart to be fucked and dumped."

"I know that." The dark, tattooed man grew quiet, lowering his gaze to the flames. "I want to know her better, and not just to sleep with. I want to understand why she's different, why she seems to be on the same wavelength as shifters when she has no abilities herself. She is just... full of purity and goodness. She's unlike anyone I've ever met."

"Same here," I agreed quietly. "Seems we like the same things about her."

"Seems we do," he chuckled. "If she doesn't want me like that, I'll be okay with it. I'm just happy to have met her."

My throat tightened, but I had to get the words out.

"Look man, if things develop between you two, that's great. Pursue it. I'm basically in love with her, but I'm one fucked up individual. I know myself well enough to admit that I won't be enough to make her as happy as she deserves. So if you can provide what I can't, great. Just take it slow. Don't push anything on her."

He gave me a long, calculated look. "And you're really okay with that?"

A heavy sigh escaped my chest. "I'm becoming okay with it. Little by little."

"Have you ever dated two partners at once?" he asked. "Or been with someone who was with you and someone else at the same time?"

"Nah," I answered. "Just seen lots of cheating and sneaking around between people who made vows to be faithful to each other. I figure if you're gonna fuck around, might as well be honest about it. You?"

He nodded. "I had two girlfriends at one point. They were in a relationship with each other, too."

"Yeah?" I raised my eyebrows. "How did that turn out?"

"The good times were... well, you can probably imagine," he said with a smug grin. "The bad times were awful, though. Three junkies together always ends terribly."

"I bet," I answered. "You seem pretty cleaned up though."

"Four years," he sighed. "Unfortunately, I'm the only one of the three who did clean up. One of them died from an overdose. The other is probably in a psychiatric institution somewhere."

"Tough shit," I said sympathetically. "Did they know about...?"

"No," he shook his head. "I snuck away to shift when I could. I had a few close calls, but they never knew." He paused, glancing over at the trailer door. "She's the only one I've felt I could be completely honest with."

"Yeah," I agreed, following his gaze. "You've just got to be brave enough to do it."

MELODY

"God fucking damn it!"

Nigel tossed his cell phone across the stage, then whipped around, looking for something else to throw while the rest of us watched silently. He settled on kicking a metal folding chair, then picked it up when it collapsed and tossed that across the stage too.

"How long is he gonna do this for?" I whispered to Connor.

At some point last night, I felt him come to bed and curl around me with all the warmth and protectiveness that made me melt in the first place. He didn't smell of alcohol anymore and he'd been cheerful and sweet this morning. His kisses and cuddles made my heart swell, but these mood swings of his always threw me for a loop. I couldn't help but wonder what was going to set him off next time.

"Just give him a minute," he murmured, rubbing a hand

affectionately across my lower back. "He needs to let off some steam. He'll be okay after his tantrum."

We all met for rehearsal at the main stage a half hour earlier. The magician hadn't shown up, but everyone figured he was hungover and would come late. We carried on without him. I'd been too nervous to eat any breakfast, but my ringmistress announcements were met with glowing praise and constructive criticism. Everyone said I needed to project my voice more, even though I already felt like I was yelling. My voice felt raw after just a few practice runs.

The magician never showed up and after a few phone calls, Nigel found out he was on a plane to Vegas for the same auditions all the others had ditched him for. Hence the temper tantrum.

"The day before opening night and he said he'd be here!" Nigel bellowed at no one in particular. "What kind of show is this without a magician?! And I paid him in advance because he owed child support! Mother fucker ran off with my fucking money!"

I snuck a glance across the stage at Razvan, who was also watching the spectacle with amusement. As if he could physically feel my eyes on him, he returned my gaze and winked. My face heated, and I lowered my eyes to the ground. Even now, I felt so bashful around him. Like he was the dreamy bad boy, and I was the loser girl with a crush large enough to have its own zip code.

But you're with Connor, a voice in my head reminded me.

"WHAT THE FUCK AM I SUPPOSED TO DO!" Nigel screamed at the sky. Razvan chuckled behind his hand at the melodramatic display.

Connor wants you to keep your options open. He's said that several times, another voice argued. That was true. Despite Connor's back-and-forth mood swings, he consistently said he didn't want me to feel tied to him.

I looked up at the sexy, green-eyed man next to me. He was watching Nigel and didn't seem to notice the not-so-subtle glancing back and forth between me and Raz. Or if he did notice, it didn't faze him.

What did they talk about last night? I wondered.

Nigel finally sank to his knees, thoroughly drained of everything he let out. Connor squeezed my waist before he let go and walked to the slumped over carnival manager. He placed a hand on Nigel's back and spoke to him in a low voice I couldn't hear.

When Nigel nodded and mumbled a few words back, Connor gave him a few encouraging pats and rose to address us all.

"We're taking a break for lunch," he announced. "Then we all come back here in an hour to figure out a routine without a magician."

Footsteps stomped off the wooden stage as everyone dispersed. As Connor made his way back to me, he wore that same grimace I'd been seeing more often lately.

"Babe, you need to lotion your legs," I hissed in a low whisper. "Forget your manly pride or whatever. They're just going to keep hurting you if you don't. You can't perform when you're in so much pain."

"I can if I need to," he growled, shooting me a glare. He grabbed my hand and we walked down the backstage steps together. He hissed in a breath when we reached the ground.

"You *don't* need to, that's what I'm telling you," I argued. "After wearing them all day, you need to bring back the circulation—"

"I know, babe. But lotion and massages are not the issue. It's just a temporary solution."

"What's the issue, then?"

He remained tight-lipped until we reached our camp, out of earshot of everyone else. Then he turned to me, placing his hands on my waist as he trapped me in that forest green gaze.

"Prosthetics need to be adjusted every few years, if not replaced completely. These are my first set and I never got them adjusted because I couldn't afford it."

"How long has it been?" I asked in a soft whisper.

"Three years," he answered. "With all the movement I've been doing, these are probably at the end of their lifespan."

I swallowed. "And how much does a new pair cost?"

"You don't want to know," he scoffed.

"Tell me." I wrapped my hands around his neck. "I want to help you, babe. We're in this together."

He sighed heavily, dropping his forehead to touch mine.

"Anywhere from thirty to seventy-five grand."

"Shit."

"Yeah. The best we can hope to make at this carnival for all nights total is ten grand. And that's a high, extremely optimistic estimate."

"Can the military help you at all?" I asked. "They're supposed to take care of their veterans, aren't they?"

"I wasn't in for long when I got injured," he said.

"What little benefits I had, I maxed out on my first set. I couldn't even tell you where my paperwork is now."

Anger surged through me. Why should it have mattered how long he'd served? He nearly died performing his duty to this country.

"Well, we'll figure it out." I pressed a kiss to his frowning lips. "We'll budget and keep saving until we have enough."

"I dunno, babe." He kicked the nearest tire of the trailer. "This thing costs a ton to gas up and maintain. I can only save enough to travel to the next carnival and keep myself from starving."

"I'm telling you we'll figure it out." I pressed my hands to the sides of his face and kissed him again, more insistently until his mouth finally opened up to mine.

Our lips and tongues made a slow, intimate dance until I felt like putty against him. His arms tightened around me, nearly crushing me to his chest as I tried my best to give him reassurance and warmth without words.

"Thank you, babe," he murmured when our lips eventually parted. "I'm so glad you're here with me. I don't tell you that enough, but you're the one keeping my head up."

My chest felt like bursting with the rush of emotions from hearing those words, from feeling him wrapped around me like a suit of armor no one could break through.

"I'm glad I'm here, too," I whispered into his neck. "You're the one keeping me safe."

His hands slid up my back as his lips brushed across my face to my ear. He just started kissing that spot below my earlobe that drove me crazy when we heard soft giggles nearby.

We both looked to our right to see Hunter in human form, holding the hands of two adorable, giggly children at his sides.

"Uh, hello," he smirked. "We could come back if this is a bad time."

"No, not a bad time! Perfect time, actually," I stammered, a giggle threatening to bubble out of my own chest. "Right, Con?"

He shot me a glare before putting on a charming smile directed at Hunter. "'Course not. We were just about to have lunch. Join us, will you?"

"If we're not intruding," Hunter said, that wily smirk spreading into a grin. Damn. He looked beautiful when he was all serious and sad, but when he smiled, he was absolutely breathtaking.

"Not at all." I untangled myself from Connor and bent over to become eye level with Hunter's children. "Hi guys, I'm Mel," I offered with a friendly smile.

"You're the lady that stealed us!" the boy declared, his pale features and golden eyes a near mirror image of Hunter's.

"The word is rescue, son," Hunter chuckled, ruffling the boy's platinum hair. "Mel introduced herself. Now tell her your name," he prompted gently.

"I'm Roo," the boy said proudly. "And that's my sister, Rinna."

The girl buried her face shyly in Hunter's pant leg, but still peeked at me with one blue eye. She was not as pale as her father and brother, and had hair almost as dark as mine up in a ponytail with a bright purple scrunchie.

"It's nice to meet you both, officially," I said. "Hopefully you've had no more scary nights like that one we first met."

"No, we went hunting with Dad again!" Roo declared, clearly the more outgoing of the two. "I caught a rabbit and Rinna helped me kill it!"

"Wow, great job!" I was honestly a little squeamish about animals getting hurt and killed, especially after learning what happened to Hunter and Razvan. But I had to remember hunting prey was part of this boy's instincts and how he would learn to survive.

"Hey, why don't you two help Mr. Connor with the cooking fire?" Hunter suggested. "Then we can have lunch." Rinna seemed to perk up at the mention of fire, but Roo's enthusiasm outshined her.

"Woooo, fire!" Roo grabbed his sister's hand and darted toward the fire pit.

"Have fun with those two," I smacked a kiss on Connor's cheek and laughed at his ensuing eye roll. But he put on a smile and knelt next to the kids, gently explaining about kindling and building a fire properly.

Hunter and I stood for a moment, just looking at each other. My face heated up with every passing second as I tried to think of something to say. Thankfully, he was wearing a shirt this time.

"They're sweet kids," I said awkwardly. "You must be really proud."

He nodded, beaming as they calmly watched Connor light the kindling and gently blow on it. "They're resilient and curious. And somehow they can still trust people. That's what really amazes me."

"Yeah. That means they'll bounce back from the damage done," I said. "Hopefully anyway."

"They were really excited to meet you," he said with a glance toward me.

"Really? Why?"

"Well, I told them about what you did, of course."

"It wasn't just me," I protested. "Connor was there, too. If I didn't have his muscle, this trailer or anything, I never would have gotten you guys out."

"He wouldn't have saved us on his own," he said softly. "I'm not sure what compelled you to do it, Mel, but you're not an ordinary human."

"I'm really nothing special," I said, fighting the rising blush in my cheeks. "I just can't stand seeing people get treated like that."

"That's the thing," Hunter said. "You *knew* we were people. Everyone else thought we were just animals."

He was right. I didn't know how I knew, but I did.

"Anyway," he cleared his throat, "do you need any help getting food ready?"

"Um, sure." I turned to the trailer door and held it open for him. "Let's see what we have."

If the trailer felt small between Connor and I, it could barely contain Hunter. He bumped his head on the ceiling and had to slouch as we maneuvered around the tiny kitchen. We laughed awkwardly and neither one of us seemed eager to address the tension with a capital T.

He lived in the forest, so how could he smell so good? I caught whiffs of clean, earthy spiciness as he moved around me. His long arms reached the top shelves in the cabinets and I saw the deep lines from his hip bones as his T-shirt lifted. And why did his slender biceps have to flex so deliciously as he brought the bowls down from the cabinet?

I saw his golden eyes in my peripheral vision like the warm, gentle glow of porch lights. I noticed how he tried not to get too close and avoided touching me. But I felt his gaze travel over me like gentle, curious fingertips, and my brain felt like it was screaming.

What are you doing, Mel? You have enough on your plate juggling Connor and Razvan! Not that you're even really seeing them both, but adding a third guy to your massive crush list is most definitely not wise.

We exited the trailer carrying bowls, utensils, and ingredients for BLTs. The fresh air and open space hit me like cool water to the face after feeling *very* up close, hot and personal with Hunter.

Connor glanced at me but said nothing when I handed him strips of bacon to skewer over the fire.

"Dad, can I shift and eat my bacon raw?" Roo asked as Hunter got them settled with bowls and napkins.

"No, Roo," Hunter said sternly. "We are guests of Connor and Mel's for lunch. They're human, so we eat with them as humans."

"You're lucky nobody heard that," Connor murmured, glancing around.

"Yeah, they don't understand the importance of keeping that a secret yet," Hunter admitted.

"I want raw bacon too!" Rinna piped up.

"Guys," Hunter sighed. "I said no. No raw meat until we're back at the den, okay?"

The kids behaved as we built our sandwiches and small-talked, but after a few bites they were already growing restless. They started chasing each other around and wrestling on the open ground near our campfire, when

Roo spontaneously grew triangular, furry ears and a wagging, fluffy tail.

"Roo, no!" Hunter bellowed with a roar I never heard in his voice before. Connor and I watched dumbfounded as he marched over to his son and picked him up by the back of his neck, which had sprouted into a furry scruff.

"Human. Now," he growled.

13

MELODY

Roo let out a soft puppy whimper and obeyed, sitting on the grass with a pout and a wobbly lip as his father spoke to him.

"Sorry about that," Hunter mumbled as he returned to sit with us. "I can't let them get away with even little shifts like that. It's way too risky."

"Little harsh, don't you think?" Connor asked, keeping his voice low.

I elbowed him in the ribs and gave him a look that said, *you're not a parent. Keep your comments to yourself.*

"For a completely human child, it would be," Hunter answered. He didn't seem offended by the question. "But we have to discipline our children like animals. I've had to keep both of them in line with my teeth before."

"It makes sense," I offered. "You have to keep them in touch with their animal side as well as the human one. Seems like a pretty delicate balance."

"Exactly." Hunter smiled at me. "See? You understand a lot more than you realize, Mel."

I thought of Razvan as a child and how he was forced to keep his dragon hidden, lest he be punished by his family. The thought made me incredibly sad for him, but also brought up a question.

"Can shifters be born from normal humans?"

Hunter nodded. "It's rare, but it's been known to happen. Sometimes the shifting genes go dormant for several generations before they appear again. Families can forget or just not know about their shifting ancestors for hundreds of years." He shoved the rest of his BLT in his mouth and swallowed in one gulp before continuing. "In wolf packs, when a baby is born without the ability to shift, we find it best to leave them at a hospital or adoption center. As difficult as it is, there's just no way a non-shifting human can fit into our dynamic and society."

"Other species might not be as kind, I imagine," Connor said.

"Very true," Hunter agreed. "There are rumors of those who kill their young who can't shift. Big cats, mostly. I've never seen it personally but I'm sure there's some truth to it." He gave both of us an appreciative smile as he stacked his and the kids' bowls. "Thank you for sharing your food and fire with us. On my next hunt, I'll bring a fresh kill to share. Any preference?"

"Venison," Connor said quickly. "I can't tell you how long it's been since I had a nice venison steak, goddamn."

"Sure thing," Hunter said. "Did you ever hunt your own?"

"I did," Connor answered proudly. "With a bow and arrows. I never liked deer hunting with guns. Too loud, too easy. I wanted to earn that kill, you know?"

"Absolutely! That's the best feeling."

The two of them started talking excitedly about hunting, swapping stories of their hunts, whether in human or animal form. I chewed my sandwich silently as I listened, watching the spark of brotherly bonding light up between them. The kids resumed chasing each other and playful wrestling, staying in human form the whole time.

They looked so innocent and happy, like they never went through such a traumatic, terrible ordeal less than a week ago. I envied their ability to leave the past behind so easily. Mine always seemed to creep over my shoulder, ready to drag me back to that hellhole if I even peeked back.

I knew I'd have to go back one day. I couldn't leave my younger siblings, some the same ages as Roo and Rinna, to suffer like I did. But I needed resources first. I couldn't go back until I knew I could take them with me, or get them to safety.

Connor's kiss on my cheek broke me out of my daydream.

"Hm?" I turned to him for a quick nuzzle.

"We were just talking about the state of the carnival," he chuckled.

"Congratulations on becoming ringmistress," Hunter said. "Women are rarely seen in such a position. I'm sure you'll do well."

"Thank you," I said sincerely. "I'm still nervous about it but practicing has helped."

"It's gonna be a rushed show, no matter what we do." Connor quickly filled in Hunter on everything we'd gone through, from the first group of performers ditching for an audition to suddenly not having a magician at the last minute. Hunter listened intently, looking more thoughtful with each passing second.

"Maybe," he stroked his short beard, looking far off in the distance as he pondered, "I could help you guys out."

Connor and I both looked at him curiously, waiting for him to go on.

Hunter rubbed his hands together and glanced back at his kids, now napping in the soft grass, before speaking again in a low voice.

"Because of what you two risked for us, I'd be willing to play the part of the Wolf Man. That way, your empty slot will be filled."

"No!" Connor and I cried out in unison so loudly that the kids startled awake.

"Absolutely not," I insisted in a whisper. "That was such a terrible experience for you. For *all* of you. We could never let you relive that again."

"Well, I don't want them involved." He nodded at Roo and Rinna, who were settling back down to nap. "They'll stay in the den. They know to stay put while I'm gone. But if it helps you guys out, I have no issue with doing a partial shift, and walking around and howling a little." His smirk returned. "My only requests are no cages and no cattle prods, although I figure I won't have to worry about that with you."

"Hunter, I really don't think I could stand to do it," I pleaded. "It would feel like I'm exploiting you. Just the thought of it turns my stomach. It feels so *wrong*."

"I'm offering to do this of my own free will, Mel," he said gently. "Remember, I'm a person too. I can make my own decisions. You're not forcing me into anything, but I feel like I owe you guys for saving us."

I turned to Connor. "Babe, please back me up. This is a terrible idea."

He placed a hand on my thigh, gently massaging around the knee. "He has a point, Mel."

"What?!" There was *no* way he was disagreeing with me on this.

"The Wolf Man act brought in a shit ton of money and a massive crowd back in Drowningville," he pointed out. "Because they hyped it up. If Hunter is out there with us and we start spreading the word now, it could turn things around for Nigel and us."

"So what, we're selling out our new friend for money?" I demanded.

"Mel." Hunter reached out and placed his hand on my other knee. The contact of both his and Connor's skin on mine was like an electric jolt. He clearly meant it as a friendly touch, but my body responded to it as so much more.

"I wouldn't offer to do this if I felt like you were selling me out," he said. "You two are my friends, and I want to help you. That's all this is."

"I can't," I shook my head. "When you were onstage, and they were so awful to you... they tortured you."

"But that's not what we're gonna do." Connor's strong fingers squeezed around my knee. "Babe, this could be a good opportunity. You could show the audience that the wolf man isn't someone to fear."

"You might be onto something." Hunter's eyes lit up. "Sooner or later, humans are going to know about shifters, and it's going to be a scary, uncomfortable reality for them. If we start by demonstrating we're not monsters, it could be a step in the right direction."

"Maybe," I said hesitantly, trying to avoid looking down at my knees where both of their hands were still on me.

"Here's an idea. We could have a secret signal," Hunter said. "I won't be able to talk, but we can check in with each other through a hand sign or something. You can ask me if I'm okay and I'll tell you yes or no."

"I would feel a lot better about doing it if I knew how you were feeling," I admitted. "If you seem even slightly uncomfortable, I'd want to put an end to it."

"It's a deal, then." Hunter removed his hand from my knee with a smile, though my skin still tingled all the way up to my sensitive inner thighs.

"Hold on, I haven't agreed to anything," I protested, trying to ignore the sensations in my body. "Can I think about this first?"

"We don't have time, babe," Connor said. "Lunch is almost over, and we're heading back to rehearse. We either tell Nigel this is happening or forget it completely. But we need to decide now."

Two pairs of eyes, gold and green, focused on me as they waited for my answer.

That's right, I told myself. I'm the ringmistress. I'm leading the entire show. This is up to me.

"Alright," I said finally. "But make sure Nigel knows Hunter is ours. He's not for sale. No one messes with him or they're dealing with us."

"That's my girl," Connor beamed, wrapping an arm around my waist. "You're learning this business fast."

I looked at Hunter. "Let's get that secret signal figured out. Oh, and you're getting paid an equal third of our cut. You're not doing this as slave labor."

"Yes, ma'am," he chuckled, golden eyes flashing in amusement. "I see what you mean, Connor. She's going to do great."

If only the knots in my stomach would disappear, and I felt just as confident as they did.

14

MELODY

One hour until showtime.

I swiped the large, fluffy makeup brush across my cheeks and did a final check of my clothes and face in the mirror.

Nigel was kind enough to give me creative freedom for my ringmistress outfit. Because most of the performers had dark, edgy styles with lots of black and dark shades, I decided to go along with that theme.

Instead of a traditional red tailcoat, I found a black cropped jacket with large brass buttons. It covered up just enough of my velvet purple corset and matched the black lace mini skirt flaring out from my legs. Sheer, lacy black stockings covered my legs, and I actually found a pair of heels that fit and felt comfortable.

And of course, the look wasn't complete without a top hat. I thought the thing looked ridiculous when Cherry first dressed me up in Drowningville, which felt so long ago. Now I swore I was getting used to the damn thing.

Satisfied with my look, I left the bathroom to find

Connor sitting on the bed and looking at a hand mirror. He was embracing the gothic theme as well, dressed in black with silver accents. He looked in the mirror carefully as he applied white face paint. Tonight he'd be wearing a black half-mask styled like the phantom of the opera.

His forest green eyes looked even brighter in contrast with the pale makeup.

"Lookin' good, mistress," he smiled approvingly as I approached.

"Hm, I like it when you call me that." I bent at the waist to give him a light kiss on the lips, careful not to mess up his makeup or mine. "Any updates from Nigel about how daytime went?"

"He was in a good mood last I checked," he said, returning his focus to the mirror. "Daytime numbers exceeded expectations so far and doesn't look like many people are leaving yet. Word of the Wolf Man spread fast."

Like back in Drowningville, the daytime carnival was considered the family-friendly event. Rides, games, sugary and deep-fried food, and children-appropriate shows. Except here, most of the daytime performers skipped out for that audition in Vegas, as did the headliners for the evening show.

So with our rushed, haphazard planning and no big names on the roster, we expected many of the attendees to leave after doing their shopping through the vendors and entertaining their children. To find out most of them were sticking around was a very good sign for us.

"We just might pull this off," I breathed with an affectionate rub at Connor's shoulders.

"It's still a snowball's chance in hell, but they may see unseasonably cool temps in the forecast," he mused.

I swallowed and decided to broach the question that had been on my mind since we started getting ready.

"How are your legs?"

"Fine."

"Con, babe. Be honest with me, please."

"I am." He lowered the mirror and looked up at me. "I had them off most of the day. And I lotioned the stubs after my shower. I'm right as rain for tonight."

My heart swelled to the point of nearly bursting. For all of this man's stubbornness and grumbling, he really did listen to me. Sometimes, at least.

"Good," I beamed, resisting the urge to kiss him again. "I know you did that because of me. Thank you."

"Believe it or not, I do like keeping you happy," he chuckled. "And it made sense. Being in pain tonight would affect the performance and I wanted to be in top shape."

"I just can't wait to get this over with," I sighed, wringing my hands together.

"Still nervous?"

I nodded. "My stomach's been in knots since rehearsal yesterday."

"You're gonna be fine, babe." He squeezed my waist. "Better than fine, even. You're going to be amazing."

"I just feel like this whole show is riding on me," I stammered. "If I screw up announcing the next act, the audience won't be hyped for them and it'll be my fault."

"That's not gonna happen." His eyes brightened. "Hey, where's your lucky coin? I haven't seen you messing with it much since we got here."

"You're right." I jumped up and rummaged through my backpack until I found that familiar piece of round metal.

I traced my fingers over the crossed daggers in the

center, then squeezed it in my palm for a few moments. I knew it was only my mind tricking me, but I felt instantly calmer with the weight of it in my hand. I placed it in the breast pocket of my jacket and smoothed my hand over it.

"There you go," Connor grinned, cupping my chin. "Now you know you can't fail."

"Thank you," I whispered, leaning into his touch. "You're my biggest supporter. There's no way I could do this without you."

"Not true." He stroked my neck in a way that made me never want to leave the trailer. "You're amazing all on your own. I'm just glad you dragged me along for the ride."

"Hey, it's not like I held a gun to your head," I giggled.

"But that ass," his other arm wrapped around my waist and slid down to grab a handful, "these lips," his thumb brushed the corner of my mouth, "and these big doe eyes." His gaze captured mine as he shook his head slowly. "How could I have ever resisted?"

"You flatter me, handsome." I thumped his chest playfully and took a deep breath. "Ready?"

"Ready when you are, mistress."

THE CROWD WAS EASILY TWICE the size of the one in Drowningville when we saw Hunter for the first time. The massive main stage and fairgrounds easily accommodated them and only made me feel smaller as I peeked from backstage.

The scene was similar, yet so different. So many more stars glittered in the sky and out here in the sticks, the energy felt... wilder. Not that this crowd was any drunker or rowdier than Drowningville, but the forest itself seemed to vibrate with anticipation of tonight's performance. There was an untamed playfulness in the air. It reminded me of Hunter's kids playing and wrestling in the grass. Innocent and harmless, but free and undomesticated.

Hunter was waiting in a private room backstage, separated from everyone else so no one would freak out at seeing him shift. He would come out last when Connor gave him his cue. And just like before, Connor would be first on deck.

The drum music started up, and my pulse thrummed along with it. In a few seconds, when the cymbals clapped, that was my cue to go out.

A hand suddenly brushed across my shoulders and startled me.

"Good luck, *steluța*." Razvan's deep rasp purred in my ear. "Not that you need it."

"Oh, believe me, I do," I whispered back. "My legs feel like jello."

"Now, I could give you a reason to make them feel like that," he said with his signature smirk and wink.

I giggled and shook my head right when the cymbals clapped and hissed.

"Knock 'em dead, beautiful," he said with a gentle push and I took my first step into the spotlight.

Just that little bit of laughter allowed me to relax enough to stride out with the illusion of confidence, and a massive stage smile for the people waiting below.

"Ladies and gentleman! Boys and girls!" I projected as loudly as I could, even with the small microphone clipped to my jacket. "Welcome to the opening night of the Crying

Falls Summer Carnival! I'm your host for the evening, Ringmistress Melody!"

The thunderous applause was shocking. I could feel the wooden stage vibrating under my feet and nearly stumbled in surprise. These people were ready to go, and I hadn't even gotten started.

"We've got a great show for you tonight and all week long!" I made sure to speak slowly and enunciate every word as I spread my arms out in a welcoming gesture.

Their unblinking eyes followed my hands as if enchanted by my gestures. A calmness settled over my limbs. I had power. I was in control.

"Our first act is a man of many talents," I said with a suggestive wink. A light chuckle and murmuring rose from the crowd, but they kept listening with rapt attention. "Handsome and strong from head to toe, this acrobatic stilt walker knows how to put on a show. Give it up for Stilts, ladies and gentleman!"

I put my hands together, and the crowd followed, sending up cheers and wolf whistles as well. As I headed off stage, I made a mental note to give Connor a better stage name. He was way too talented for something so dull.

My heart practically vibrated in my chest as I went behind the curtain, still riding high on the crowd's energy.

"Holy shit," I breathed. That went so fast, I could hardly believe it actually happened. I did it. I really fucking did it.

"Good thing your mic's off," someone remarked.

I blinked until my eyes adjusted to the darkness of backstage. Nigel stood there with a beaming grin that rivaled the sun.

"How'd I do?" I asked, feeling some panic rise.

"How do you think you did?" he shot back.

"Um, good?" I swallowed and straightened up taller, holding onto the power I just held while looking into hundreds of pairs of eyes. "Good. It felt really good."

Nigel sighed and shook his head, my confidence withering.

"Melody, you weren't just good."

"Oh... no? I—"

"You were fucking brilliant."

I blinked, thoroughly confused. "Really?"

"Girl, you cast some sort of spell out there. They were mesmerized by you. Now Connor's riding off that magic, too. Look."

Together, we peered past the curtain to see open mouths and wide eyes glued to Connor as he did flips, handstands and backbends. A sharp pang pulled at my heart as I watched him. He was doing the same amazing solo act he always did before me, but I missed performing with him.

Being ringmistress felt incredible, but it was different when I was on that stage with Connor. It was like an intimate dance, an expression of trust between us. And a testament to how well we worked as a team as long as we both put forth the effort.

Holy shit, I'm in love with him.

"Well, I suggest you tell him that, girl," Nigel chuckled.

I looked at him. "Did I say that out loud?"

"You sure did."

Thank God for thick stage makeup, otherwise I'd be as red as a tomato.

"Well, keep being the best goddamn ringmistress I've

ever seen, and then tell him," Nigel laughed. "I don't want you distracted and all googly-eyed. We've still got the rest of the show to put on."

"Yes, sir," I giggled. "How's the turnout, by the way? Still above expectations?"

He hissed in a breath and closed his fists with determination. "I don't want to jinx it, but if your wolf man is legit and you keep working your magic like that, I don't think we'll have anything to worry about, sweetheart."

"That's great news!" I grinned at him. "We won't let you down, Nigel. Promise."

"Well, we still have a whole week to see if there's a drop-off. I don't want to get too optimistic but..." He trailed off, grinning uncontrollably. "At least for tonight, you've really turned this ship around, Mel. Connor's a lucky man."

"I'm the lucky one," I whispered, watching proudly as the crowd gasped at his stunts.

I didn't let him listen to my announcement about him during rehearsal. I wanted to surprise him, to shout out to the whole audience what I really thought of him. And I meant every word. I just hoped he knew that.

The crowd burst into raucous applause as he performed his finale and took his final bow. His eyes caught mine from across the stage, but I couldn't read his expression. I blew a kiss anyway before he stilted off to the opposite end of the stage. I wanted to chase after him and kiss him properly, but while his part was over, I still had work to do.

"Mic's on. You're up, mistress," Nigel cued with a wink.

I strode out into the light, all my nerves gone and my

smile one of genuine pride. My confidence no longer felt like a mask. It was real, and this show was mine.

"Let's give it up for Stilts one more time, ladies and gentlemen! How incredible was that?"

Their applause sent another burst of energy into the air, a single united sound from hundreds of hands and voices. The power practically vibrated over my skin.

"Stilts is always popular with the ladies," I said, strutting across the stage like I owned it. "Now we have some lovely ladies for you gentlemen in the crowd!"

The burlesque troupe came out next, putting on a highly entertaining show full of old-school tasteful stripteases with a dash of comedy and light magic tricks to keep everyone engaged.

It was Nigel's idea to keep everyone hooked with high-energy acts, followed by calmer, more low-key performances. Every high-energy stunt grew bolder and more shocking as the evening went on.

Soon it was time for Razvan's troupe, who would combine fire breathing and sword-swallowing into one act. And then it would be Hunter's turn to shine.

I took a sip of water, already feeling the stress on my vocal cords, before stepping out once again. "I don't know about y'all," I said, turning up my country accent. "But we haven't seen much *fire* tonight yet, have we?"

The crowd screamed, mostly the men, and raised their fists in the air. Most of them were good and drunk by now and enjoying the hell out of themselves.

"That's what I thought," I said knowingly, looking out at everyone. "We're turning up the heat now, ladies and gentlemen! Our next act loves to live dangerously! Whether by flames, sharp objects, or both at the same time. Give it up for the incredible, death-defying Flaming Swords!"

I barely turned to walk off the stage when two shirtless, heavily tattooed men came running out like ninjas. They dashed onstage, juggling swords in the air while moving with lightning speed. Only when I went behind the curtain and turned back to watch did I realize they were blindfolded.

"Holy shit," I breathed. These guys were *good*.

Two more blindfolded men walked out, and the crowd went nuts with screams. These two juggled a pair of fiery torches like it was a walk in the park. They weaved in and out with the sword jugglers in perfect synchronized form. The stage lights went low to enhance the dancing fire of the torches and the flash of metal from the swords. Everyone was stunned, including me.

But still no sign of Razvan.

I watched the show feeling entranced but couldn't help the sting of disappointment. Where was the sexy, smooth-talking leader of these daredevils?

"He'll make an entrance when you least expect it," said a female voice from behind me, as if she could read my mind. "He never fails to blow everyone away."

I turned and recognized Ally, the girl who'd been sitting in Razvan's lap when I first went to speak with all the acts. Her face was heavy with makeup and she was still in her lingerie from the striptease she performed earlier with the burlesque show.

"I wouldn't put it past him," I said with a smile, biting back the unexpected jealousy that flared up. "He's great at what he does."

"He's great at *everything* he does," she purred, popping

her hip out to one side and placing a hand on it to empha-size her point.

I kept my face friendly, resisting the urge to narrow my eyes into a glare. What right did I have to be possessive about Razvan? She and he were together in some way.

You're the only human here who knows he's a dragon shifter. That means something.

"I bet," I said lightly. "You're his girlfriend, right?" I kept my tone casual, despite my insides seething for reasons I couldn't explain.

"You could say that." Her lips curved into a smug, wicked smile. "He's *definitely* off limits."

I forced out a laugh. "Don't worry. I got my own man who's plenty enough to handle."

"Good." Her blue eyes flashed challengingly. "You don't seem like the type of girl to steal another's man."

Apparently, you haven't met two bitches named Cherry and Leeann, I thought.

"I'm not," I assured her. "Connor makes me really happy."

That was the truth, despite the uncomfortable tight-ness around my heart from learning Razvan wasn't actually available. For a moment, I was beginning to think all his teasing and flirting meant something. That *steluța* meant something. But my first impression turned out to be right. He was just a shameless flirt and sweet-talker.

I looked back out to the stage. The jugglers had just finished a routine, their swords or torches in each hand as they froze in a kneeling position. A heavy silence hung over the stage and audience. With Raz's guys like statues, everyone seemed to be holding their breath for what was to come next.

And then a *creak* came from the rafters above my head.

I looked up just in time to see a blur of inked skin fall from the stage's ceiling. A scream threatened to escape, but my throat was too dry from announcing. Razvan landed lightly on his feet, tilted his head back and exhaled a massive orange flame.

15

MELODY

People screamed and backed away from the stage, but the burst of fire from his lungs dissipated within seconds. Only the flash of heat on my skin remained. If I could feel it from back here, I could only imagine how those in the front row felt like.

With that charming grin, he pulled his hands from behind his back to reveal two long, gleaming swords. In the next moment, the twin blades lit up into flames and the fast-paced music kicked up again.

Razvan moved so quickly, my eyes could barely keep track of him. His crew resumed their blindfolded juggling, pausing only to engage in lightning-fast sword battles with him and each other.

His flaming swords cut like liquid through the air. I'd never seen anything so beautiful and entrancing. Metal clashed and clanged. Sparks flew as fire met fire.

There was no way all of this came from his shifter abilities. The fire breathing, sure. But the speed and precision with which he moved amounted to years and years of practice.

He used to be forced to do this, I remembered sadly.

Why did he keep doing it then? Why didn't he seek out other members of his kind to live freely with them? How did he go through every day not feeling like he was in a nightmare?

His face only showed that signature cockiness and playfulness. More women in the audience started pushing toward the front, wanting to get closer to the fire breathing, tattooed bad boy. One particularly drunk woman lifted her shirt, flashing a pair of breasts that were much bigger than mine. Razvan paused to blow her a kiss before continuing with his act, and her friends dragged her away.

Does he know her? Who is she?

I looked back at Ally, who caught my gaze and just rolled her eyes.

"He loves the attention, but he'll learn that I'm all he needs," she said.

Bless your heart. Keep telling yourself that, girlie.

I learned early on—from everyone my mother brought home—that men were creatures of habit, not change. I lost count of how many times they swore up and down they'd support her and never bail, but that was the first thing they did when she got pregnant. How I figured this out at fourteen while she never seemed to was completely lost on me.

Even knowing this, the discomfort wrapped around my heart only squeezed tighter.

Returning my attention to the show, I realized the music and Razvan gradually slowed down. He waved the flaming swords hypnotically in a figure-eight motion in front of his face, shifting his body from side to side in a way that was downright erotic.

He paused, holding one sword vertically in front of his face for just a moment, then tossed it straight up in the air.

People screamed again, some covering their heads and moving away, others keeping their eyes glued to the long shaft of metal in the air as it sailed up, and then began its return down to earth.

Razvan dropped to one knee, spread his arms to the side and tipped his head back, sticking his tongue out like a snake. Wait, was his tongue forked? I'd never noticed it before.

A perverse thought filled me for a half-second, flushing my body with heat and arousal, and then the sword dropped.

The long, fiery metal blade seemed to slide down his throat in slow motion. I couldn't believe my eyes and wanted to cover them, but at the same time couldn't look away.

Everyone in the audience reacted similarly, by covering their eyes or mouths. He remained kneeling, unmoving for a moment, with the cross-guard resting on his lips. Then he raised a hand. With hundreds of eyes tracking his movement, he wrapped his fingers around the handle and rotated the sword ninety degrees.

"Oh god, I can't watch!" someone cried out.

Razvan raised a middle finger in the direction of the voice, eliciting laughs from everyone else. It eased the nail-biting tension in the air for a moment before continuing with his act.

He raised his other hand, the second blade still alight

with flame like a beacon on the dark stage. His long, tattooed arm lifted the sword as high as he could before tilting it down to point at his mouth.

"Holy shit, two swords?!" someone cried in disbelief.

His realization was confirmed as Razvan smoothly lowered the flaming blade past his lips, tongue, and throat. He made no sound, nor any movements that showed discomfort or pain. He might as well had been holding a spaghetti noodle.

I thought back to the moment I first saw him practicing, juggling those small knives, and how I screamed when he caught them in his mouth. I had no idea then, but on that stage I realized the knives had been child's play.

He spread both arms wide to his sides again and rose to his feet, head still tipped back, and two sword handles resting on his lips. The crowd broke out into thunderous applause, the loudest standing ovation I heard yet. They yelled and whooped and hollered at the top of their lungs, amazed by the human wonder standing before them.

How would they react if they knew this man could shift into a giant, flying reptile? Would they even care if he was free or enslaved?

Razvan raised his fists to his mouth and removed both swords at the same time, their flames now extinguished. With a sweeping flourish, he bent deeply for his final bow, raising another wave of thunderous applause and screams.

The click from the microphone pinned to my jacket was my cue to go out for the last time that evening. I took a few deep breaths to compose myself after what I just saw, then put on my smile and walked out.

"Give it up for the Flaming Swords, everyone!" I boomed.

The crowd was fired up. Some were even yelling, "Encore! Encore!" But we had to move on. It was time for Hunter to come out, and my stomach was in knots once again.

Razvan laughed, giving another sweeping bow and blowing kisses out to the audience as he sheathed the swords on his back. Then his arms went around my shoulders and waist so fast I didn't have time to react.

He dipped me low, supporting my back. I saw his steel-colored eyes flash intensely for a moment before he kissed me.

I kissed him back before my brain could catch up to what was going on. My body reacted on instinct and once that forked tongue flicked gently inside my mouth, I only craved more.

But then it was over just as quickly as it began.

He broke the kiss and pulled me back up to standing, a wily grin on his face as he held my hand aloft in his.

"Give it up for Melody, our beautiful ringmistress, everyone!"

The crowd cheered and whistled as I smiled and laughed. I waved and said, "Thank you so much!"

But my mind raced at a mile a minute. My heart spun in my chest with confusion and desire.

And behind me, I felt Ally's glare like a dagger in my back.

16

HUNTER

A gentle knock rapped at my door.

"Yes?"

It pushed open, and Connor stuck his head in. He still wore the white face makeup, but pushed the black half-mask to the top of his head.

"You're up next, Wolf Man."

"Thanks, Connor." I stood from the chair to prepare for my shift. "Sorry," I chuckled with a bit of forewarning as I made off with my shirt and jeans. "I have to undress or I'll ruin these clothes."

"Uh, right." He looked pointedly at the ceiling. "No worries."

"How's it going out there?" I asked while I could still speak.

He let out a low whistle and shook his head in disbelief. "Mel is killing it, as we knew she would. The crowd's only getting bigger and crazier with every act. We're about to be over capacity for the main floor and people are watching from the lawn." He shot me a teasing smirk. "No pressure or anything."

"I'll be fine," I said with a shrug. "I won't be watching them, just hurrrgh."

My throat and vocal cords shifted and rearranged as my teeth grew into sharp points and my tongue elongated. White fur rippled across my entire body. My ears moved up the sides of my head and pricked forward and back when I flexed the small muscles attaching them to my skull. My tail and claws had grown out, but I stopped the shift to remain standing upright.

"Ready, man?" Connor asked.

I barked an affirmative in reply, then followed his lead out the door.

He led me through a dimly lit corridor. Through the walls, I heard voices of the crowd screaming and stage hands shouting directions.

"This is a private hallway," Connor explained. "No one will see you. I'll stay with you backstage in case anyone decides to get nosy."

I softly barked my gratitude, hoping the message would get across with my lack of a human mouth. To my surprise, he chuckled and held out his fist.

"No problem, buddy. It's the least we can do."

I bumped his fist with the back of my paw and resisted the urge to lick him. He was a good human, one of the rare few I'd met in my life. The other was his beautiful lover up on that stage.

In my drugged-out haze back in Drowningville, I remembered seeing her face from the stage. While everyone else's were blurred and distorted, her face stood out clearly. Beautiful and sad. She'd been crying when she saw me, but not out of fear. It was like she saw through my fur and teeth and could feel my pain as if it were her own.

I never dreamed they would rescue us, but before I passed out, I felt an inkling of hope. There was at least one human out there who didn't see us as monsters.

And now I knew there were at least two.

Connor led me up to the backstage area. He directed me to a corner where I could remain hidden in shadows but see both the front and back of the stage. I caught the show just as the other shifter put on his fire breathing display.

"You good, buddy?" Connor asked.

I bumped his fist again and looked up just in time to see Mel walk out from the opposite side. My heart skipped a beat in my chest and my ears pricked forward. If she had any nervousness left, it didn't show. She walked out on long, shapely legs like a model on a catwalk. Her full lips and dark eyes beamed with delight and natural beauty. Whether onstage, backstage, or the audience, there was no head she didn't turn.

"Give it up for the Flaming Swords, everyone!" she declared.

Surprise rippled through me as I watched the kiss between Melody and the dragon from my backstage spot, but I wasn't nearly as shocked as the other dark-haired girl with her mouth hanging open in shock.

"I'm gonna kill that bitch," she whined as she stormed off.

My hackles raised, and my teeth bared in her direction. No one fucked with Melody without going through me. And I knew of at least two others who would stand up for her as well. I learned of the second one just then upon witnessing that kiss.

The audience hooted and hollered like it was all part of the show, and maybe it was in a small way. But I smelled the dragon's desire the moment she walked onstage. Apparently, they had gotten better acquainted since I watched them walk in the woods together. I wondered if Melody saw his dragon form yet.

I sensed that he was reptilian, but the fire he breathed gave proof to something I'd never thought I'd live to see. A mythical shifter, here in the backwoods of Mississippi?

Running into other shifters was rare enough, but there were estimated to be less than twenty dragons in the world.

I slid a questioning glance over to Connor as Mel and the dragon breathlessly parted. He seemed even less surprised than me.

"It was bound to happen," he said with a shrug. "I'll explain it all to you later, but I'm fine with Mel seeing other people. As long as they're good to her, of course."

I nodded, letting out a soft *whuff* of agreement. It only surprised me because humans seemed so insistent on exclusive pairs.

Multiple lovers were fairly common in wolf packs. An alpha female often took several male betas as mates. Beta females could have more than one mate as well, with the permission of the alpha. My mate had me as her primary, but found comfort in others when I went on long hunts. It kept her happy and distracted her from worrying about me.

"I have a very special guest joining me for our final show tonight," Mel declared as the dragon and his men exited the stage. "Some of you may be frightened at first, ladies and gentlemen. But I assure you there's nothing to fear! My friend is gentle and kind, even if he may look like a fearsome beast. But he's also a person with intelligence and emotion. He can understand words and ideas just as well as you understand me now."

She walked across the stage with firmness and intention as she spoke, making sure to look directly into people's eyes as she did so. Damn, Connor was right. She *was* killing it.

"My dear ladies and gents, let this be a friendly reminder to not judge a book by its cover. Or a tiger by its stripes or a wolf by its teeth." She paused, letting their silence and rapt attention hang in the air like a fog. "Without further ado, I give you my incredible friend, the Wolf Man!"

"Go get 'em, man," Connor whispered with an encouraging slap on my back.

I huffed in reply and took my first steps out, letting the stage lights fall on me and keeping my eyes trained on Melody's.

I expected some anxiety as I walked across that wooden stage, hearing the gasps and cries in my ears. But as Melody's warm eyes and smile grew closer, I realized I had none at all. I'd never been on stage like this—free and not in a cage. By my own choice and not dragged in chains. By being greeted by a friend who said kind things about me.

A friend who risked her life to rescue me and my children.

Melody winked at me, our secret signal. It looked cute and flirty to the audience, but she was really asking me if I was okay. I answered yes in the way we agreed, by flicking my left ear twice.

Satisfied, she returned her attention to the audience.

"No need to be alarmed, ladies and gents. My friend here wouldn't hurt a fly. Well," she passed a grin over the dumbfounded stares, "maybe if a fly was on his dinner."

I licked my lips when she said dinner, and the crowd noticed. We rehearsed quickly earlier in the day. She would prompt me to do things or I would respond to words so everyone could get through their thick heads that I wasn't some dumb beast.

"Hmm, I'd really love a better view of the Ferris wheel." She looked out across the audience to the carnival rides in the distance. "Would you mind giving me a boost, Mr. Wolf?"

I lowered myself to her level, wrapped an arm around the backs of her legs, and raised her up to the height of my shoulder. The crowd gasped in unison, as if I was King Kong with the delicate damsel in my grip.

But Mel was completely relaxed as she sat on my bicep. She draped an arm around my shoulders and gently scratched the fur there. My pulse picked up. It had been ages since anyone but my kids touched me affectionately. I barely remembered what the touch of a woman felt like.

"Thank you, Mr. Wolf. The view is much better from up here."

I howled my agreement. It really was a beautiful view. Romantic, whimsical, and dark.

After a few moments, I gently lowered her back to the ground.

Dare I? I thought.

Before I could think too much, my tongue darted out

and licked her face. That wasn't scripted, and panic jolted through me. Did I go too far?

Mel just laughed as she pressed a hand to her cheek. "Aww, you're so sweet, Mr. Wolf," she said.

The crowd finally began to relax, laughing lightly at my lick and talking in hushed murmurs among themselves.

I was amazed at how at ease she seemed. She was either an amazing actress or she really was as comfortable with me as she was acting. Being in-between shifts was often grotesque-looking to us as well, not just humans. But Mel was smiling and blushing with me just as much as she was with Connor or the dragon.

She faced away from the crowd for a moment and winked at me. I flicked my ear twice, and she nodded.

"Do I have any brave volunteers who would like to meet my friend, the Wolf Man?" she asked the audience. "Remember, he is a person and will be treated respect-fully, not ridiculed. Otherwise," she stepped directly in front of me and reached up to scratch my jaw. Oh god, that felt nice. "You'll have to deal with me," she added wickedly.

Pride and warmth swelled within me that I hadn't felt in years. It brought me back to having a mate who defended me and had my back at every twist and turn.

I wrapped a protective paw around Mel's waist and let out a soft warning growl. It didn't matter if she was my mate or just a friend. If she had my back, the least I could do was have hers.

Some audience members backed away from my bared teeth. Others stood frozen. No one seemed to be in any particular hurry to join us onstage. The silence dragged on and Mel stepped away from me, standing like she was about to make her closing announcements, when a small voice piped up.

"Can I meet him?"

Everyone turned in the direction of the voice. A girl no older than eight with wide blue eyes looked fearlessly into mine. My heartstrings tightened. Her eyes reminded me of Rinna's. She pulled against the hand of her mother, who looked just as stricken with fear as everyone else.

"It's alright, ma'am." Melody smiled kindly at the mother. "My friend won't hurt your child. He adores children."

"Yeah, for breakfast!" someone called out, eliciting snickers from his companions.

Melody and I ignored them and the girl only pulled harder against her mother, who allowed herself to be dragged a few hesitant steps forward.

"I just want to pet him, mommy," the girl said. "He looks like a doggy."

"That's right, sweetheart," Mel encouraged, stepping closer to me again. "And he's as gentle as one too."

"You swear?" the mother croaked in a harsh smoker's voice, eyes narrowing on Melody. "You swear to God almighty it ain't gonna eat my kid?"

"I swear in Jesus' name, ma'am." Mel placed a hand over her heart. I didn't take her for the religious type, but she was eager to placate the mother.

The girl dragged her mom all the way through the barricade and up the steps at the side of the stage. Mom kept her hand tightly wrapped around her daughter's. Her expression of fear mixed with disgust never changed.

I stayed back as Melody went to greet them at the end

of the stage. She knelt in front of the girl and asked softly, "What's your name, sweetheart?"

"Amy," the girl answered.

"Would you like to make a new friend today, Amy?"

The girl nodded, looking over Mel's shoulder to meet my eyes again. She smelled similar to Mel. Fearless and brave. Completely human, but with a touch of something different.

I allowed Amy to approach me, lowering my head and wagging my tail encouragingly. Her mother remained at the edge of the stage and looked ready to run off, daughter or no daughter.

Mel held Amy's hand as she reached out and scratched under my jaw again with the other. Goddamn, that made me just want to stretch out in her lap and bask in her sweetness.

"You can pet him like this, Amy," she said gently.

Amy reached out with a small hand and gave me the softest scratch on my forehead. I leaned into her hand and licked her fingers, thumping my tail emphatically on the stage floor.

"He licked me!" she giggled, smoothing her hand over me with more confidence.

"That means he likes you," Mel told her.

"You're really soft," Amy said, looking directly into my smiling jaws. "Is it okay if I hug you, Mr. Wolf?"

The question took me aback for a moment. For one thing, she asked *me* directly. Not Melody. Everyone else spoke to Mel as if I wasn't capable of understanding, despite her proving to them otherwise. Everyone except this brave little girl, who was like a miniature version of Mel.

I nuzzled my face close to hers and opened my arms. Amy loosely wrapped her hands around my neck and rested her face in my fur, while I gently placed my paws on her back.

A soft chorus of "*Awww*" rose from the crowd. Maybe they were finally getting it.

I licked Amy's ear, tickling her as she giggled and squirmed away.

"Give it up for Amy and the wolf, everyone!" Melody declared as she led the girl back to her mother, who promptly whisked her off the stage.

The applause that rose was quieter and more hesitant than it had been all evening. People looked as if they were confused, unsure of whether to trust their own eyes or the knee jerk reaction of fearing the unknown.

Good. That meant they were thinking.

Mel and I stood facing the crowd as she delivered her closing announcements, encouraging people to tell their friends and come back for more throughout the week. We did our final bow and this time, people let loose on their cheers and applause. The moon hung full and bright and I let out a howl for a last little bit of showmanship. That got howls and wolf whistles in return.

Mel shot me a wink as we walked off stage together, but it wasn't a secret signal this time. Her broad, beautiful smile told me that much, and my heart skipped a beat.

We made sure everyone saw us walk off the stage together, side by side as equals.

17

MELODY

Hunter shifted to human the moment we had privacy backstage. As soon as he did, I jumped on him with a hug.

"Holy shit, that was awesome!" I laughed, squeezing my arms around his bare shoulders. "You were absolutely amazing! Did you see all their faces?! And that little girl was sooo adorable."

The discomfort on his face confused me when I pulled away.

"Hey, you okay?" I asked him, concerned.

"Um, sorry," he said, his eyes glancing down. "I can't wear clothes during a shift and uh..."

I followed his gaze and promptly jerked my eyes back up to his face, but it was too late. I saw. And I couldn't unsee.

"Oh no, I'm sorry!" I stammered as I grew uncomfortably hot. "Uh, I totally should have known."

"No, don't worry." His blush on his fair skin was beyond adorable, and it only made me hotter and more uncomfortable. Fuck a cold shower. I needed to be dropped into an ice bath.

"Here buddy, I got you."

Connor walked up out of nowhere, pushing a bundle of clothes into Hunter's arms. Both of them sighed in relief as the tension dissipated ever so slightly.

"Thanks, man." Hunter pulled on the clothes quickly while the strongest pair of tree trunk arms swept me up in a crushing embrace.

"You were incredible, babe," Connor murmured before kissing me deeply.

My mind was whirling up until that moment. Razvan's kiss confused me but set me on fire. It was at the back of my mind the whole time I was onstage with Hunter, who I also seemed to have an incredible connection with. Not to mention I just saw him naked, and what a sight *that* was!

But all that melted away when Connor lifted me up and stole my breath from my lungs. In this moment, it was just me and him. The uniquely beautiful, loving dysfunction that was *us*.

He kissed me like nobody was watching, like Hunter wasn't right next to us fumbling to get dressed and like Razvan's kiss didn't even matter. This was *our* moment.

My heart crashed so hard against my sternum, I had no doubt he could feel it. His own heart beat in time with mine through the thin cotton of his shirt. I wanted nothing more than to wrap my legs around his trim waist and find a private place. When we broke apart for air, his wild, forest green eyes told me he had similar ideas.

"I'm so proud of you, babe." He peppered kisses across my face and neck, his hands beginning to roam across my body. "I knew you could do it."

"Thank you, my love." The endearment slipped out and panic temporarily froze me.

But Connor only grinned and pulled me in to capture my mouth again. His length, already thick and hard, pressed against my hip and my core flooded with heat in response. He took a firm hold of my wrist and nipped my earlobe, eliciting a sharp hiss and then a light moan from me as he teased the spot on my neck just below it.

He began pulling me in the direction of our trailer, and I was eager to follow. I turned to say goodnight to Hunter when we saw Nigel running up to us. He wore a grin that looked like he just won the lottery.

"Amazing job, everyone!" he cried jubilantly. "Especially you, Mel! I'm still crunching the numbers, but this was a record-breaking turnout! We've got to celebrate! Drinks are on me!"

"Uh..." Connor gave a side-eyed glance to me, which I returned with a half-hearted eye roll.

"We should celebrate and mingle, babe," I told him, then looked over at Hunter. "You should come too and bring the kids! There's food and non-alcoholic drinks in the tavern."

"Yes! The more, the merrier!" Nigel turned to Hunter as if noticing him for the first time and stuck his hand out. "Hi, I'm Nigel. Carnival manager at your service! Are you a friend of Mel and Connor's?"

"You could say that," Hunter replied with an amused smirk.

No one but Connor and I knew what Hunter looked like in human form. We figured he'd be safer that way. We just told Nigel we had the Wolf Man from Drowningville to fill in the empty slot and, because he had nothing more to lose, thankfully took us at our word.

"Well, lucky you getting a backstage view! How about that wolf man, huh? Mel really knows how to woo a crowd." He turned back to us. "Seriously, bring all your friends! Drinks are on me for the whole carnival crew and their people!"

"And he wonders why he can't afford his mortgage," Connor mumbled when Nigel darted away.

"Oh, be nice." I smacked him playfully. "He really has helped us out a lot."

Lacing my fingers with Connor's and Hunter walking on my other side, the three of us followed the crowd of carnival staff to the tavern. The guys talked excitedly about the acts and performers, even making crude jokes about the burlesque show that had me rolling my eyes. Men.

They seemed to have a rare friendship spark, those two. I looked between Hunter and Connor and saw the same animated expression in their faces, just from talking to each other. It wasn't that they were leaving me out, I was just content to listen. All the talking in my ring-mistress role today drained me, and I was happy to be quiet for a while.

I also kept my head on a swivel to look out for Ally, and by association, Razvan.

Why did you have to kiss me, damn it? I demanded silently. *And why right then? Your timing is sure impeccable.*

I could still taste the heat of his kiss, even now after getting swept away by Connor's kisses. Raz's mouth tasted like a fresh cup of hot coffee at just the perfect temperature. Warm enough to bite, but not quite hot enough to burn.

There was no sign of either of them as we entered the tavern, and a confusing mixture of disappointment and relief swept through me.

Confused. I seemed to be feeling that way pretty often lately.

Was I reading into Hunter, pulling out a chair for me and smiling? Was he just a gentleman, or did he feel that same fluttering in his chest when our eyes met like that? It didn't matter if he was human, wolf, or in between forms. Something about those golden eyes and that lithe, strong body just captured me like prey.

"I'm going to get the kids," he said, brushing his fingertips along my elbow as I sat down. "Save us a spot?"

"Of course," I smiled up at him. "Do you want us to order for you?"

Hunter told us his requests and quickly left. The moment he was gone, Connor slid an arm around my waist and kissed my temple.

"You want him too, babe." He wasted no time in getting to the point.

I looked at him, eyes filled with guilt. "Is it that obvious?"

"With how googly-eyed you two were at each other, I think you convinced Nigel he was your boyfriend and not me."

"You're not my boyfriend. You've made it clear you don't want that," I said, more snappish than I intended. "We keep talking about this, Connor, and I feel like it's going nowhere."

"Shush, babe. This is a night of celebrating. I'm not

trying to upset you." He took my chin in his hand, gently turning my face to his. "I've thought about it some more and I think I've sorted my feelings out."

I raised my eyebrows expectantly. "And?"

"I'm in love with you."

Everything went still. The crowded, noisy bar faded away to nothing, and all I saw was Connor's handsome face.

"What?" I barely spoke at all, just mouthed the word. I couldn't have heard him correctly.

"I love you, Mel." Every syllable out of his mouth carried nothing but raw honesty, straight from his heart. He meant every word, and I didn't know how to handle that. No one had ever meant it when they said those words to me before.

"I want you to be happy and to have whatever—and whoever—you want. Nothing less."

He leaned his forehead gently against mine. "You won't always want to be around me, and understandably so. I know myself well enough that I won't make you happy all the time. Even though I do love you, I'm not perfect. If you'd rather spend time with Razvan or Hunter, I'll understand."

"Hunter? I... maybe." Admitting it felt heavy and real. But who knew if that was even what Hunter wanted? "Nothing's going to happen between me and Razvan, though," I said with a shake of my head. "So you can forget about that."

Connor narrowed his eyes in confusion. "That's not the impression I got from him kissing you."

"I was talking to his girlfriend literally seconds before that happened! He basically cheated on her with me in front of a crowd of people, and now she definitely hates me. Who knows what his deal is, but I don't want any part of their drama."

Connor rubbed his jaw. "I dunno, babe. There might be more to this than you think. Maybe you should just talk to him."

"If he wants to talk, he knows where to find me," I huffed. "Oh by the way, I love you too."

He grinned broadly and pulled me into a kiss that slowly began erasing Razvan's memory from my lips. I'd never betray the dragon shifter's secret, but I didn't need him. Not like this. With Connor and potentially Hunter and his kids, my heart was full enough.

"*Now* can I call you my boyfriend?" I asked when we parted.

"Alright, fine," he sighed with mock frustration before he chuckled and kissed me again.

Our food soon came out, covering the entire table. Connor and I started digging in when Hunter and the kids showed up. I had no idea I'd been so hungry. Today had taken everything of me.

"Ooh, ribs!" Roo declared as he pulled himself up to the table.

"I want ribs too!" Rinna piped up.

"There's plenty to share," Hunter sighed with an eye roll, but smiled warmly at them.

The five of us talked and laughed into the night as we ate and drank. Rinna began coming out of her shell and told me about the butterflies she chased through the field that morning. Hunter looked overjoyed that she was talking to me without any coaxing. The poor girl probably hadn't talked to any women since getting captured.

Hunter had one beer, kept carefully out of the kids' reach, but I noticed Connor didn't order any alcohol.

My boyfriend was in a flirty mood, kissing my cheek and teasing me at every opportunity, but not possessive like he usually was. When Hunter and I got into a conversation, he engaged with the kids, telling them jokes and funny stories.

When our bellies were full and my eyelids started to droop, Hunter took the kids to the restroom. I watched them as they walked away, the family that had been through so much but still managed to look out for each other.

"So, what do you think?" Connor wrapped an arm around my waist, pulling my back against his chest and dropped a kiss to my shoulder. "Want to spend more time with the wolf family tonight?"

In that moment, there was no question of what I wanted.

"No," I said, looking up at him. "I want to go home with you."

His eyes flickered with pleasure. "You sure?"

I kissed under his jaw, pressing my ass into his crotch to make my intention known.

The time to explore something with Hunter would come. And with his children to consider, if anything progressed between us, it would need to go slowly. I was fine with that. I wanted everyone involved to be aware if things developed between us.

But right then, I didn't feel like exploring anything new. I wanted familiarity, the comfort of the man I knew and loved.

"Goddamn, girl. We have to wait and say goodbye first," he teased, nipping at my neck.

When the three wolves came back, we passed around celebratory hugs and goodnights. Hunter was so tall, I had to stand on tiptoes to reach around his neck. He squeezed gently around my waist and our embrace lingered, like neither of us wanted to let go.

"Thank you again," he whispered in my ear. "For everything."

"No, thank you," I smiled as I pulled away. "You saved all our asses tonight and gave us a reason to celebrate."

He gave me one last heart-melting smile before taking Roo and Rinna's hands in his. "See you two around soon."

Connor and I followed them out the door, our fingers intertwined between us. We barely walked ten feet when an anguished cry and a slap rang out.

Our heads snapped over to see Ally and Razvan in the middle of a heated argument. Her face red and streaked with tears, his fists clenched at his sides.

18

MELODY

"Enjoying what you've done, bitch?"

Ally turned to me, her jaws clenched with rage and heavy, sobbing gasps of air coming from her chest. She lunged toward me, spurring all three men into action.

Connor jerked me behind him, Hunter stepped up next to him with a protective growl. And Razvan grabbed Ally's arm, preventing her from getting any closer. A red mark on his cheek showed that he'd been the receiver of the slap a moment ago.

"This has nothing to do with her," he insisted, pulling Ally back by her arm. "Don't drag other people into your petty shit."

"Look at this smug bitch!" Ally screamed, gesturing wildly. "One guy isn't enough. All three of you are being fucking white knights. It's fucking ridiculous!" She turned a poisonous glare to me. "You lied to my face! Are you seriously fucking all of them?"

"Stop this nonsense. You're hammered." Razvan

wrapped her in a bear hug and began dragging her away. He shot me an apologetic look. "I'm sorry about this, *steluţa*."

"I'm not the one you should be apologizing to," I fired back, stepping in front of Connor. "Ally?"

"Fuck you, bitch!" she twisted in Razvan's tattooed arms to shoot me another hateful glare.

"I didn't lie to you," I said, ignoring her insult. "I don't steal other women's men. But you have to remember that men make their own decisions." My gaze flickered from Razvan back to her, trying to ignore the memory of his lips on mine and that split tongue caressing mine. "You can have him, Ally. Although I think you could do much better."

I turned to continue walking, pulling Connor by the hand with me. I didn't want to see Razvan's face. It hurt me to shut him down like that, even if it was the right thing to do. I didn't want to think about the possibility of hurting him, too.

"Was that really necessary?" Connor asked after we said a final goodnight to Hunter and the kids and continued on the path to our trailer.

Our trailer. When did I start thinking about it like that?

"Doesn't matter now," I muttered. "I don't want to think about that."

"I think it's worth it to hear him out," he said gently. "Maybe after a few days, once y'alls heads are cleared."

"You two really bonded during your late night talk, huh?" I gave him a sideways glance.

"Sort of," he muttered. "He gave me a good perspective on things I didn't think about. Even before Hunter came along, I was starting to think he'd be good for you to turn to when you don't feel like dealing with me."

When we reached the trailer, I playfully shoved him against the door before he could open it. Like a good sport, he allowed me to pin him there, humoring me with a grin.

"Well, that time is not right now," I said in what I hoped was a seductive whisper. "Not another word about Raz or Hunter."

"Yes, ma'am," he grunted, lifting me up under my thighs. His mouth claimed mine as my legs wrapped around his waist.

Now in control, he turned us around and pressed my back to the door. His hips rolled against my heated core, already revved up and ready to receive him.

"Fuck me, babe," he moaned into my neck as he fumbled with his key and the door.

"That's the plan," I whispered hotly, scratching my nails up his back like a cat scratching at a post.

We finally made it inside, and he sat us down with a heavy groan on the bed.

I paused for a moment. "You okay?"

"Babe, my legs could be bleeding, oozing stumps and with you wrapped around me like this, I'd still be okay."

"Mmm, super hot imagery for when I'm right about to fuck you," I teased.

"Call me a magician," he teased back, working my jacket off my arms. "I can bring your mind back to a state of arousal. *Abra cadabra*, just like this."

My breath caught in my throat as he pulled my hips tight against his hot, pulsing erection. The pressure and hardness made my clit explode with sensation and beg for more. Combined with his gentle sucking right below my earlobe, I temporarily forgot my own name.

"Connor," I moaned, squirming in his lap for relief.

He held my body captive and tight against him, his strong arms pinning me to his chest as he moved just slightly. They weren't thrusts, just slight rocking of his hips and we still had all our clothes on, for fuck's sake. But the pressure right on my aching clit, the friction, how hard he was and just how tightly he held me, caused the first orgasm to rip through my body.

I shook and convulsed and whimpered and only after all that subsided, did he loosen his hold and I slumped limp like a rag doll against him.

"A gentleman always makes his girl come before she's even naked," he chuckled with a kiss to my cheek.

"I thought you were a magician," I whispered breathlessly, pulling at his clothes.

"Why not both?" His voice became muffled as I peeled his shirt over his skin.

His arms slid around me to deftly pull apart the laces of my corset. With all my senses heightened from that orgasm, I glued myself to him and just drank in his bare skin on mine. Every scar, muscle, and bone told a small piece of his story. I watched my own fingers trail across his arms and chest in magnified concentration. I wanted to know this man every night down to the smallest detail.

My corset came off, breasts and ribs spilling after being caged in that thing for so many hours. Connor lovingly kissed and massaged my tender flesh, bringing cries of relief bordering on pain as circulation returned to those areas.

We untangled for a moment to remove pants and

underwear. He stopped me when I went to peel off my stockings.

"Leave those on for me," he said with a soft rumble. "You look so sexy wearing nothing but lace on your legs."

"Oh? A fetishist, are we?" I teased, slowly crawling back into his lap.

"I dunno," he shrugged. "It's just hot as fuck seeing you with a little bit of clothing still on." His powerful arms went around me again, crushing me to the hot, solid wall of his chest. "I still love you naked, though."

"They're coming off as soon as we're done," I said with playful warning.

"Mm, then I might have to fuck you again." He made a trail of kisses down my neck and across my shoulder. "You know, for science."

His talking became wordless moans as my pussy rubbed against him. Heat building more heat, my soft to his hard. I lifted my hips, beyond ready to impale myself on him, when he stopped me.

"Condoms, babe," he reminded me with a kiss.

"Oh, right." Embarrassment flooded through me for forgetting.

I laid on my side, watching as he went to retrieve it from the shelf. Just enough light filtered through the curtains so I could see just the shape of him, the contours of the well-defined muscles adorning his body. They tensed and coiled with precision at every little movement he made—ripping open the package and sliding the rubber onto his length.

A fresh rush of heat flooded my core as I watched him touch himself. He gave himself a few strokes back to full hardness and tugged at his balls with a soft groan. I'd have to remember he liked that.

Without warning, he flipped me over onto my stomach and pulled me up to my knees. A sweet tingle erupted over my scalp and his mouth fanned a soft breath on the back of my neck.

"You like this, baby?" His fist wound tighter in my hair as his teeth tested the soft flesh of my neck.

I gasped, my back arching with need. I didn't even realize I backed toward him until I felt his round head kiss my slick, swollen entrance.

"Yes," I whimpered. "Oh please, Connor."

He surged forward, spreading me apart with a hot moan. His fist tightening in my hair as he pulled back, his other hand digging into the flesh of my hip.

He thrust into me so deliciously. I loved it, coupled with the light tingles of pain from his hand in my hair and his bites on my neck. He moved both hands to my waist as he fucked me, but I wanted more.

I craved it, needed it.

"Spank me," I begged. "Connor, please."

"Well, damn," he grunted, delivering a few wonderful smacks on either side.

I hummed with pleasure and begged for more, pressing back into his thrusts for more of him inside me. I couldn't get enough. He obliged until my ass stung and I felt a familiar pressure building in my clit.

Connor noticed the change in my moaning and picked up the pace and force of his thrusts. His hip bones pressed into my ass as he reached forward to soothe the ache in my stiff nipples. I saw stars when I came, my pussy closing around a rod of concrete that suddenly jerked with a convulsion of its own.

"Fuck," he groaned with his own release, fingers digging into my hip as he nearly fell forward.

The next sensations I felt were his kisses on my back, followed by the emptiness of him withdrawing from me. I wondered if I passed out for a moment.

Connor collapsed on the bed with deep, ragged breaths, and I curled up into his side. The comfort of his arms around me and his rapid heartbeat underneath my ear were everything to me in that moment.

"I didn't know you liked that rough stuff, babe," he said, smoothing his palm over the tender flesh of my ass.

"Me neither," I said with a shy giggle. "You pulling my hair just felt so good. I was craving more of that feeling."

"I'll remember that," he said with a kiss on my forehead. "Damn, we gotta get you on the pill," he sighed. "I wanna feel you bare."

The thought of feeling his orgasm spill inside me, with no barrier between us, was incredibly hot. Especially if it didn't mean an unexpected child later on down the road.

Thinking of children brought my attention back to Hunter. If we pursued this connection we had, I'd be basically dating a single father. What would that be like? How would the kids take it? Were there unspoken rules for dating men with kids? I'd never really dated anyone before, certainly not anyone I felt as strongly for as these three men.

Damn it. Not Razvan too, I cursed within my head. I had to let those feelings die. He was not someone I wanted to get involved with.

Weariness settled into my limbs and I snuggled harder

against Connor, who was already breathing rhythmically. I had a feeling not many humans knowingly dated shifters, or vice versa. It was uncharted territory for all involved. We'd tackle challenges when we got to them.

One dick at a time, I thought with a giggle.

Whatever happened with Hunter and everything else on this roller coaster, I'd have Connor beside me. Even if he made me crazy, I knew now his love was genuine, and he was just as crazy about me.

EPILOGUE

RAZVAN

Fucking Ally.

Fuck her and her drunk, dramatic ass starting shit. I should have nipped that in the bud right away. Now I had a mess to clean up.

I hated having to take care of her drunk ass, but if I didn't, there would be two possible outcomes. One, she'd go after Mel and, at best, start some petty girl fight. At worst, she'd seriously hurt Mel with how fucking pissed off she was. Just in my trying to restrain her, she scratched me hard enough to draw blood. Better me than Mel on any day.

The second possibility? Some asshole, or worse, a gang of them, would take advantage of her in her drunken state. I wouldn't put it past some of these rednecks, nor would I wish that on Ally or anyone.

I couldn't allow either or both of those things to happen, so I spent the night keeping her away from Mel instead of being with Mel myself.

I saw her through the doorway of the tavern with

Connor, a couple of kids, and some pale guy I hadn't seen before. One smell of the air and I knew he was the wolf. Ah, so he emerged from the shadows at last. I couldn't catch his act because of dealing with Ally, but the buzz around it was nonstop. As the attendees left, that was all they were jabbering about. Good. The final act had to be the one that stuck in their mind.

When they left the bar and I saw the look in her big brown eyes, I knew she had already written me off. And that hit me in a deep, hidden place I often forgot was still alive.

I shouldn't have kissed her. Not onstage like that.

Did I regret it? Hell fucking no.

Was I going to make this right? I was going to try my damn hardest.

The other burlesque dancers were too busy with their own hookups to babysit Ally, so I had to stay with her throughout most of the night. An exhausting, infuriating night of her throwing up, mumbling curses about Mel, then shamelessly trying to fuck me.

"I hope you remember this because I'm not coming back here," I growled, pinning her wrists away from me for the tenth time. "It's over between us, not that there was anything to begin with. I'm not fucking you anymore. I'm fucking done with your bullshit."

"Whyyyy?," she wailed. "What's so special about herrrrr?"

"She doesn't act like this, for one fucking thing," I mumbled, rubbing my temples. I could very quickly appreciate that Mel didn't drink at all.

I couldn't stop thinking about her being with Connor right then, the sounds and faces she made as she expressed her pleasure. My dragon fired up with jealousy and it was all I could do to keep him at bay.

I fucked up. Connor was who she rightfully wanted and needed at that moment. I had to set things right and then show her she had nothing to fear by choosing me.

The day was young by the time Ally passed out. When peaceful silence finally greeted my ears, nothing sounded better than an early morning flight. It was risky, of course, but still dark enough that no reasonable person would be awake.

But that didn't stop me from seeing if someone would still wake up and join me.

Cool morning dew clung to me as I took the short walk to Connor's trailer. I didn't expect to see the light of his campfire, but also wasn't entirely surprised.

"Mornin'," he greeted from his lawn chair.

"Ah, good morning," I answered, noticing something else that took me by surprise.

He wasn't wearing the metal legs he showed me. His legs ended in stumps, one right below his knee, the other halfway down his shin.

"Close your mouth or you'll swallow a fly, Raz," he mumbled, sipping coffee from a mug.

"I'm just... even more impressed with your acrobatic abilities now," I said, running a hand over my short, buzzed hair. "I mean damn, man. Be honest, how fucking hard is it?"

"My dick? Well, give me a few minutes to refract and wake up the lady," he laughed. "The stilt shit? Yeah, took some adjustments. My training in the Marines helped, though."

I nodded. It didn't even bother me anymore that this

man was fucking Mel maybe minutes ago. He lived through a hell that killed other humans and for that, he had all my respect.

"I actually came over to see if you could wake her up," I said. "I've been up all night and might as well watch the sunrise with someone I'd like to spend time with."

His eyes narrowed, and I saw that protective tension ripple over him. "You've been up doing *what*, exactly?"

"Just making sure the girl didn't get raped or come out here to fight Mel," I said, feeling just a hair defensive. "Nothing happened and there was nothing between us, really. We fucked once, and she got attached. I never promised or committed to anything. And now I let her know nothing will happen again."

Connor visibly relaxed. "I figured it was something like that, but that girl made it sound to Mel like you two were dating. She's not too happy with you, man."

"Exactly why I want to straighten things out. So what do you say, Connor?" I grinned sheepishly, trying to curb my eagerness to see those beautiful, dark eyes again. "Let me take her to see a romantic sunrise?"

He rubbed his jaw as he thought, turning his gaze to the trailer door.

"I dunno, man. Nothing against you, but I feel like she needs a bit more space. The next morning is still fresh, you know?"

Fuck.

"Sure," I said, my dragon roaring his protest inside me. "I don't want to force anything and make it worse."

"Give her a couple of days, then come back," Connor said. "Trust me, I've been keeping you in my good graces, but she's a stubborn one."

"Don't I know it." I laughed. "I get it. Thanks, man. Guess it's a solo flight this morning."

"Flight?" Connor raised an eyebrow.

"Oh, that's right," I laughed. "I never told you straight out." I took one glance around at our empty surroundings. "Well, fuck it. Hope you're not afraid of giant, flying lizards."

I began the shift before he could react. When it became clear what I was doing, he grabbed his armrests and nearly leaped out of his chair. I would've felt bad if he had fallen out, but he thankfully didn't. He was nearly as accustomed to seeing this as Melody.

"A fucking dragon?" he whispered hoarsely when my shift completed, his eyes nearly bulging out of his head. "Fuck, I should have known," he laughed with a disbelieving shake of his head. "Fire breathing, of fucking course."

I snorted with laughter, smoke curling from my jaws and nostrils. With a derisive nod, I pushed off the ground and took one powerful beat of my wings to get airborne. Connor, his trailer, and the whole world became tiny versions of themselves within seconds as I ascended higher and higher.

The sky was still dark except for a creeping sliver of light on the horizon.

One day, I thought. *You'll be sitting on me, wild and free. And we'll see this view together.*

THANK you so much for reading *Abra Cadabra!* Book 3 in the series, *Smoke and Mirrors, is available now!*

NEWSLETTER & READER GROUP

Never miss a book release, plus get three *free* short stories when you sign up for my newsletter!

Grab your freebies at:
crystalashbooks.com/freebies

You can also join my reader group on Facebook to get updates and hang out with fellow readers.

Join Crystal's Coven at:
facebook.com/groups/crystalscoven

ALSO BY CRYSTAL ASH

Say Your Prayers

Shifted Mates Trilogy

Unholy Trinity: The Complete Series

Harem of Freaks series

Steel Demons MC

Lawless

Powerless

Fearless

Painless

Helpless

Heartless

Senseless

Ruthless

Merciless

For a complete list of books by Crystal Ash, visit her Amazon page.

ABOUT THE AUTHOR

Crystal Ash is a USA Today Bestselling Author from California. She loves writing steamy, heart-wrenching romance with tortured heroes, especially if they're in a reverse harem. Crystal's other loves include animals, mythology, and well-crafted alcohol, most of which can also be found in her stories.

When she's not writing, she's probably drinking craft beer with her husband or trying to coax her feral cat into accepting affection.

crystalashbooks.com

facebook.com/Crystal.Ash.Romance

instagram.com/crystalashbooks

amazon.com/author/crystalash

bookbub.com/profile/crystal-ash